WHITE OUT

WHITE OUT

a novel

MARTINE DELVAUX

Translated by **Katia Grubisic**

Prepared for the press by Carmelita McGrath
Cover image: Éléonore Delvaux-Beaudoin
Cover design: Debbie Geltner
Book design: Tika eBooks

Library and Archives Canada Cataloguing in Publication

Delvaux, Martine, 1968-
[Blanc dehors. English]
         White out / Martine Delvaux ; translated by Katia Grubisic.

Translation of: Blanc dehors.
Issued in print and electronic formats.
ISBN 978-1-77390-001-8 (softcover).--ISBN 978-1-77390-002-5 (HTML).--
ISBN 978-1-77390-003-2 (HTML).--ISBN 978-1-77390-004-9 (PDF)

         I. Grubisic, Katia, translator II. Title. III. Title: Blanc dehors. English.

PS8607.E495B5213 2018   C843'.6   C2018-901368-0
                              C2018-901369-9

Printed and bound in Canada.

The publisher gratefully acknowledges the support of the Government of
Canada through the Canada Council for the Arts, the Canada Book Fund,
and Livres Canada Books, and of the Government of Quebec through the
Société de développement des entreprises culturelles (SODEC).

We acknowledge the financial support of the Government of Canada
through the National Translation Program for Book Publishing, an initiative
of the *Roadmap for Canada's Official Languages 2013-2018: Education, Im-
migration, Communities*, for our translation activities.

Linda Leith Publishing
Montreal
www.lindaleith.com

This is the end of the story, and the beginning. How does it feel, I get asked, not to know who my father is.

I'm eight years old, ten, twelve, I don't know, I don't remember. I'm lying on my bedroom floor, bent over a pad of paper, long white pages, lined, probably, one of those outsized notebooks we used back then for accounting or to keep track of inventory by hand. I'm lying on my stomach on the red and orange rug in my bedroom down the hall, at the back of the bungalow, windows overlooking the garden behind the house and beyond that the forest, dark and deep, woods where I have never been. My knees are scored by the long synthetic fibres that scratch and itch. It's probably summer, humid and warm, the summer of mosquitoes and of the hairy spiders I find on my bed, and I'm bored in this house stuck by a highway, this strange place where nothing ever happens, hay fields in summer, and in winter snow to the end of the world. I've covered an entire page of the notebook in my awkward handwriting, hiding the words so no one can see, and now I'm transfixed, staring at the paper in silence, waiting for the words to come alive, for the air to become magically different. There, it's done, the words have been written. I have written them.

But life goes on, nothing moves, I'm still alone in the room.

I don't know anything because I've been told nothing, or almost nothing, and anyway nothing good, nothing substantial, nothing worthwhile. All I know is that he left a long time ago, before I was born. He left because I was going to be born. He couldn't do anything to change that, and my existence in this world was something he wanted nothing to do with. He didn't ever want to run into me. Cross the street, turn away. I stormed into the world, that much I've been told, over and over again, my life is an accident, an obstacle across the path of that man, across the road my mother took, and which he chose to avoid.

The little girl lying on her belly on the rug is writing to him, scrawling sentences that don't ask who he is, why he's not there, why he left. She asks no questions, she doesn't know where to start, or how to address him. Sir, To whom it may concern, Daddy? She asks nothing, and tells nothing. She threads one sentence after another like mysteries between her fingers. Her child's words are a hesitation between seeking and forgetting, between ascribing meaning to the word father and abandoning it, lost in the dictionary.

The letter is put away in a box deep in her closet and one day she takes it out to reread it, centuries later, when she's decided that the story has to be written once and for all. She becomes weary, dizzy, nauseated. She recognizes the page but not the words. Her body remembers writing them, each one of her senses remembers, and yet, today, rereading it, all she wants is to turn away, become a stranger, forget that face of hers.

She remembers she was alone in the room when she wrote it, and that she was suddenly embarrassed, as if someone were spying on her and she had been caught red-handed. As if she were guilty of having dared to write him.

The letter was a life preserver and the words were sonars, like the call of submarines, or whales or dolphins, music that bumps into what hides in the dark. Words like wind. Blank words, white words. The little girl wrote the words and afterward she put her head down and covered the pages with her body. So that no one would see, and so that she too would forget.

I've been circling this book just like I've been circling all my life around this story told over and over again, and each time I keep my mouth shut, taking up the same words, the same flat phrases, always coming up against the wall of how little there is to say, and, worse, against the absent words, the vanished words, transparent, forbidden. Not allowed to say anything. Not allowed to ask. No one can tell me who I am, and those who know pretend not to. It must remain unsaid, let's forget what happened, and in that gap between what was known and what we can say, there she was, that little girl. She was told early on that her father had left, but even though the truth wasn't exactly kept from her, she understood that she wasn't supposed to talk about it. They looked off into space or turned away when she even breathed a word about the subject, when she couldn't help it or when she suddenly wanted to get a rise out of them or a stunned silence, when suddenly she might ask, Where do I come from, how did I get here? She was like a judge, her questions a trial.

That was the law, implicitly. Never say anything. To speak meant to suffer.

I learned to repeat the same phrases, like old men who chew over the same thing on a loop, broken minds grasping at leftovers, musical phrases, a cruel sing-song reminder that writing is a crime far worse than speaking, because to write is to carve. The text is another body, the driven nail of my presence here. In spite of herself the little girl had a body marked by the traces of the man who left, her colouring especially, her pale skin, the green eyes. Her mother's sharp tongue when she told her, Your hair is yellow like his. The little girl quickly understood that it was better to go unnoticed.

Later, when she's older and trying out her voice, it's always the same story that stutters out of her mouth, a disorganized tumble of sounds because the words won't come, or those that do aren't the right ones, it sounds wrong, she falters, it doesn't flow, she doesn't recognize her voice. The only words that are true are those spoken in silence.

I hover between indifference, sadness, shame, and rage. Like night-lights left glowing in the bedrooms of children who are afraid of the dark, or like the dancing blue flame of a stove, I'm in sleep mode. All my life I've always been able to remember everything—details, a glance, words, inflection. As if I had been gathering proof against forgetting. I didn't understand how or why but suddenly it all began to disappear—a thought I'd just had, a movie I'd seen, a book, a conversation. I started having memory lapses. I had to keep starting over, there were no more words, there was no grammar anymore. My infallible memory, which used to stand guard, is going idle.

I can no longer remember anything, I say things that I erase right away, I no longer create memories, I don't even know what I could write. My mind has become the house of John Sloane, walls covered in paintings hung over each other, opening up like skins lifted and peeled until all that's left is a draft wafting from room to room like the flesh of the body opened up to read the story written inside, to find the scene of the crime, the place where pain is hidden. A small place, a secret place.

Maybe all I've ever done is use words to fill in the blanks.

I'm searching for the right key. I've been looking for months. I don't know anymore who's speaking in this story, if it's mine or if it belongs to others. But I can't wait for people to die before writing, I will write for the living and with those around me. I will write—ashamed to tell, afraid to hurt, but especially terrified of failure. I can barely hear the sound of my own voice. I'm tired. I can't help it. I close my eyes.

Life goes on, ordinary, its to-do list and errands. Years speed by, books get written anyway, so many pages compared to those I don't write, that story on the scaffold of a thousand omissions, which now I have to write otherwise I never will, and the story will never exist.

He left so that I could write.

December, 1968. A hospital room. A raging snowstorm. That's what I know.

In the room there is a bed and on the bed there are sheets, a blanket, a mountain of creases. That's what the photo shows, and in the centre a young woman with dark hair, a pixie cut, tendrils flicking her cheek. She sits on the bed with her back against the pillows and cradles a baby, round-faced, a bit red, the skin of the newly arrived in the world, small fingers stretched out toward her with the animal awkwardness of newborns, and her fingers brush up against the baby, a light, delicate gesture, a little distant.

She is young, she is beautiful, I've always found her beautiful. Her face is calm. She isn't crying. She's not smiling either. The picture shows her profile, she is turned away from the camera, bent over the baby she holds in her arms. She seems to be thinking. She seems to be elsewhere.

Already, there she is and there I am. She's the one who is becoming my mother.

Tracking shot. I'm twenty years old, as old as my mother in that picture. I'm in the downstairs bedroom at my mother and stepfather's, a house I've never lived in.

9

I'm in the bedroom where guests sleep when they come for a few days, and where I sometimes spend the night.

My mother is standing in front of me, holding a white plastic basket filled with laundry to fold. The light is dim, the window is small, the room is half dark. I've come over to pick up a few things and for a last family meal before I leave. I'm leaving the country tomorrow. My mother knows this is when she will lose me, and that in the coming months she will have to live with the fear of losing me even more, and maybe forever—danger, the unknown, her hands shaking during rare calls from old rotary phones at the back of dive bars in lost villages in Ireland or Corsica or along a deserted highway. Her insomnia. It's the night before I leave, and that night she tells me that maybe, since I'll have crossed the ocean, I'll want to go looking, find out where I come from, stir up ghosts, roll back the stone. Today all that is left is for her to offer me what little she knows and has kept buried inside her until now, rare pearls held against forgetting.

What she doesn't know is that I don't want to go looking. Lack of courage has finally won out over curiosity. I have no hope anymore and looking for him seems both futile and impossible. Deep down I believe there's nothing to find, I can't find anything because I would be looking for something that no longer exists. My mother has no idea how utterly impossible it is for me to picture myself in a library or archives, or in a government building, with some official, a detective or a lawyer, up to my elbows in records. The task seems so large as to be endless, and I can't do it. I can't draw, I refuse to drive a car, and I can't track down my father. The search takes place in my imagination. Reality won't change anything. It is something else entirely, something that has nothing to do with reality.

That night, my mother leans back against the door, and I stand in front of the oak bookcase with its Time Life series on lost civilizations, a set of volumes from when my grandmother worked at the fabled encyclopedia publisher Grolier, *The Accursed Kings* with their quilted blue leather covers, a slightly damaged copy of *The Godfather*, a testimonial from a woman recounting her rape, the farm novels my great-grandfather published, and Marguerite Duras's *L'Amant*, which no one here has read but me.

My mother speaks and time stops. The time is now, never before, and never again. We are twins staggered in time. I listen, I drink in her words, silently, hanging on to catch every last drop, immobile as a birdwatcher, still and frightened that the bird might fly away. In one hand I hold a piece of paper and in the other a pen. I write down how old he was, where he came from, where he lived, what he did for a living, what he looked like, where they met. My mother's face is broken, scarred by real concern, real sorrow, tormented by the remorse of having destroyed the only image she had of him, a photo that might have told me something, a picture she tore up to turn over a new leaf, starting her own life anew by erasing my history.

She waits, watching me intently, but at the same time her eyes seem downcast.

I remember the urgency, all was not lost, my desire still sparked, it wasn't over. A moment of panic. Catching the words like a child running after soap bubbles to grab them before watching them burst. I scribble things down without thinking, I document my mother's story though I know this moment will pass and soon she'll go back to her silence, and I will be sent back to my forgetting.

No book has ever been harder to write. I'm constantly hesitating, changing my mind. I get caught up on nothing, attached to nothing, I dissolve, dissipate, I move all the pieces around and the versions multiply, I run around in all directions without being able to land, avoiding the screen, and meanwhile tension creeps into my shoulders and my back, my hands cramp up. I don't want to hurt others, and above all my mother, so I carry the pain. My mother, to whom I've always been loyal, despite rejection, conflict, absence, anger. She is the person I've wanted to protect above all, and above all from me, respecting her silence, caught up in the admonition to live with things as they are.

I've always been afraid I would hurt someone and regret it. And I've always been afraid of losing face, this face that isn't entirely my own but one I wear as if it belonged to someone else, the face of the man who chose not to be my father.

My face is a poorly fitting mask, off-set, off centre, and stuck to my skin. A mask that looks like this story without words, which is and is not mine.

Among my working titles for this book, scribbled and then crossed out, liked and rejected and in some cases liked again, titles like borrowed names, names exchanged, imposed, and impossible to adopt: *The Orphan Book*, *The Bastards*, *A Geometry of Souls*, *How to Dress a Ghost*, *Beauty Lies Sleeping*, *Behind My Back*, *Every Woman Loves a Fascist*, *The Father Who Never Was*, *The Curse*, *Gone Baby Gone*.

I'm twenty. I'm standing in the ground-floor guest room. My mother is almost silent. She doesn't have a lot of words. She's not moving, somewhere between despair and pride. An iron maiden. She almost looks like she's wearing a corset, or maybe a suit of armour. Her body is coiled in anticipation of the task ahead, her body stiff, thrust between the past and the future—a past she can't turn to and a future perpetually escaping, a sifted horizon.

What she finally says is almost nothing, scraps I've kept in the kraft paper envelope I've carried around for years and boxes filled and emptied, filled and emptied in a litany of cities and countries, neighbourhoods, houses, rooms. Words read over regularly, occasionally, less and less often, aware each time that everything has been forgotten since the last time. Forgetting doesn't change anything, because words don't tell the truth, they don't offer me anything concrete to lean on, nothing that even looks like an origin. Ancestors. A heritage. Roots.

It begins with a foreign-sounding name that can be spelled different ways. This she tells me right away, she doesn't know how it's spelled, how he wrote his name, and I jot down the name and its variants at the top of the page, a question mark in the margin. A name I don't know how to spell—how can I be sure it's the right one, whether what my mother remembers is real, whether the young man told her the truth at the time?

My mother doesn't say very much, her memories are vague, like survivors of a shipwreck washed threadbare by the salt. I can't remember what comes before this scene, or after. A few details have stayed, and I don't know anymore if even those are true, if those words were really spoken or if I made them up.

My mother stands in the guest room. I don't recognize her. Head down. She seems smaller than I am. My mother speaks, she is barely twenty years older than I am, my mother, her younger self sweeping over her, a different face closing over like a sliding door, her life fragile under the hard shell that's allowed her to survive her own mother's intransigence, cold and rigid, my ruthless grandmother who never forgave her anything. That young girl's face is what she has worked so hard to forget, the obedient smile in old pictures, her short, slightly backcombed hair, kohl-lined eyes, the multicoloured tunics, my mother the dreamer who wanted to be a beatnik, who read Freud; my mother, coy, shy, and quiet, my asthmatic mother, my mother sketched out quickly, a few quick lines drawn around her revolt.

I see her in my mind, bent over a book, a pen in her mouth, in her school uniform, I see her thoughtful, cigarette in hand in front of a bottle of Coca-Cola, dark curls, her eyes serious, a pale, melancholy curtain.

There was something of my mother in a character who haunted me for months before I wrote what I'm trying to write. I was trying to write other things, pages to elude the silence, other pages that had everything to do with the ones I'm filling now even if I didn't know it then, I couldn't, I was too tethered to reality to see it. I had just had a crazy love affair that had ended badly and there was some connection between my romantic disaster and the story of my mother, her heartache and my complicated arrival, impossible things to grieve and around which I was still going in circles, me and those with whom I was living, like the souls of those who die by suicide and continue to roam like insomniacs around the living.

I was writing one scene, always the same, telling the same story over and over again, I was orbiting around it, fascinated. It was the story of an actress, very young and very pretty, who had become an overnight celebrity at the same time as her marriage to one of Hollywood's best-paid actors, much older than she was, the circus of their engagement atop the Eiffel Tower, a black diamond, a pregnancy, the kind of man who always gets what he wants, especially women and especially that particular woman, very young and very pretty, the chosen one he suddenly placed at the centre of his life.

From the door of their luxurious hotel room, we see her lying in an enormous chair curled up in the fetal position. He set her like that after lifting her off the floor like a child sleeping, or a young husband carrying his bride. Earlier that evening, when he stepped toward her with his fist raised, his eyes ablaze, maybe she told him coldly, without trembling, like Julia Roberts to Clive Owen in *Closer*, I've been hit before. And maybe that's what set him off, his rage greater still because he wouldn't be the first.

They're shooting in Paris, they've brought their little girl. She's sleeping in the next room, and that night, just before sunrise, after champagne, bottles of Saint-Émilion, vodka, maybe even weed or pills, he lifted his hand against her, once, twice, three times, again and again until she is where she is now, curled up on the couch. For a minute, maybe she felt his presence there still, stumbling and stunned like it had been another man than him who had just knocked her around. In his drunken state, seeing his wife beat up on the floor, maybe he mused that the body is a funny thing.

As the city wakes the next morning, her picture is everywhere, on newspaper stands and in barroom windows, larger than life, a photo taken the day before the incident. The actress is walking along de Rivoli holding her daughter's hand. Next to that picture is another, smaller, of him, handcuffed between two police officers.

I was tossing words up on the screen, I was writing something, but I couldn't get through it. I kept coming back to that woman lingering between life and death, I couldn't let go of her, couldn't kill her off or wake her up, and finally I was exhausted and I abandoned her, feeling like I had betrayed her. I gave up, this wasn't it, my heart wasn't in it, this wasn't the story I was trying to tell. I needed something else, whatever was beneath, and which I could not see. My mind was an expanse of white. I didn't know what to write anymore. All that was left was invention, which is to say, lying. There would be truth only in what I would end up spinning.

Tracking shot. I'm forty years old. My grandmother, my mother's mother, is lying in a hospital bed in Montreal. I'm standing in the hallway with my back against the wall. My uncle is with me, my grandmother's son, my mother's brother, the oldest, the favourite. He paces in the hall while orderlies wash my grandmother's body, which is almost completely still, a body still living and almost dead. A body that's lived so long that the heart, exhausted, has nearly stopped beating.

Standing in the hallway, I ask my uncle if he remembers where I was born.

I don't know why I ask the question right then, I don't know where it comes from, from what corner inside me, but the words come out, my grandmother is going to die, my second mother, and soon there will be no one left around me.

I ask him only this one question. I don't ask him how he felt about it. I don't ask him if he resented his family for changing his life like that, invaded by his swollen-bellied little sister. I don't ask him if he saw an opportunity to defy his father yet again. These are all things I've already explained to myself over the years. Nor do I ask him if he was happy to hear of the impending birth. I only want to know where I was born.

I hear him answer, Jeffery Hale. He pauses, adds, They said it was the Jewish hospital. I think that was it.

He furrows his brow as he speaks, the memory isn't clear. The hardy, high-spirited boy has become a man, heavier and older. I watch him search for shreds of the past. He sees himself as a student or as a young worker, an editor at a schoolbook publishing house, writing poetry on the back of an envelope. He's a young man who likes to travel, he's recently married, his young wife is gentle and sweet, the parents are happy with the match, they feel fulfilled, proud that their son has done well.

He leaves me in the hallway and goes back into the bedroom, sits on a straight chair next to his mother's bed. She is asleep, that sleep that is the antechamber of death. I only stay a moment, I note the name of the hospital on an old receipt dug out from the bottom of my purse. I don't how to spell it, I've never heard of it, I don't know Quebec City. I've never really spent time there. I only know the ramparts, the cannons, the Saint Lawrence River, the cobblestones.

My grandmother died the next day.

She was a hard woman, cold and stubborn, often callous, unable to compromise, fiercely intelligent even until death—the battle a part of her was determined to win. Don't give up on life, don't let death win. Put death to death. When she was forced to capitulate, because death was stronger than she was, she screamed—gruesome, terrifying screams, her body jerked up on the bed, lifted off the pillow by a surge of life, something desperate, half-breath, half-scream, as if she were furious, and then she fell back, it was over, the room was suddenly empty. All the air in the room had been sucked out with her last breath and suddenly I couldn't breathe. I went out into the hallway, living was meaningless.

Death is never gentle. There is always a murder, and my grandmother's life had just been stolen. Her body had been conquered, but she wasn't ready to die, she would never have been ready. That was the horror of her wild cry, her body screaming scandal. It wasn't like in the movies, a breath so soft you had to put your ear to their mouth to hear it. Death was carnage. I wanted only one thing: for it to stop, for her to stop having to look death in the face. I wanted the waiting to stop, to stop waiting with

23

her, and despite everything to stop hoping, because as long as there is some life, it's death that is in mourning.

She liked to say how she used to rock me to sleep.

My grandmother is a very old woman. She's worn a wig for years, since the morning she woke up to find her hair had fallen out. She picked hair off her pillow by the fistful. All that was left on her head was a thin white cloud. I once asked what had made her hair fall out. A big stress, I was told.

She would have been about forty. I count back, and wonder about the timing of my mother's pregnancy.

My grandmother has been wearing the same wig forever, since before I was born, and she'll wear it until the end of her life, though it's ridiculous that a woman her age has hair that colour. The wig doesn't age and it makes her look fake, eccentric. There's something embarrassing about that relationship to time. I know it doesn't fit, but when I look at her, that's not what I see. As far as I'm concerned, that is my grandmother's hair.

She's ninety-five, and the hospital staff tries to calm me down by telling me kindly what I've already understood, the time has come. Her heart fought the good fight but now her limbs and her lungs are slowly filling with water. The pauses between breaths draw longer and longer. For days I stay by her side surrounded by the grim noises of drowning. The doctors speak in euphemisms: there's nothing left to do, nothing to be done, it's over, I have to let her go.

I was watching her sleep once from the foot of her bed when all of a sudden she opened her eyes and asked, When are you leaving? Another time, a voice boomed over the intercom and she jumped in her sleep. Eyes closed, she said, We are in the right place.

For days I cool her forehead with compresses, I feed her tiny spoonfuls of broth, I place droplets of water in the hollow of her cheek, and then on her lips. I do this until the very end, because, as long as death has not arrived, we have to take care of the life that continues to beat in the body. When the time between one breath and the next stretches so long that I begin to wait for the last one, when death has become a vigil, I stroke her hand and tell her a story as you would to a child, like my grandfather used to tell me, early in the morning when both of us waited for my grandmother to wake and he made up tales of adventure or outlandish safaris for me.

I tell my grandmother that she and I are on vacation in some grand hotel, that we have come here to rest. I choke back tears. I say the things we say when we don't know what to say because what there is to say can't be said. You can't tell someone that the time has come to die, you can't say it's time to let go, because you love them and because death is unbearable, even if the pain of seeing someone go

26

is unbearable too, and then shame sets in before a silence too heavy to carry, when you want to quell your own pain, your own treachery.

I couldn't stand to watch her die anymore.

One night, I'm thirty, I've just had dinner with my grand-parents, and my grandmother, reacting to some random story or to an anecdote she heard from one of her widow friends, tells me she never suffered from depression, but that, if she had, it would have been when my mother told her she was pregnant. I listen to her without speaking, so they can't tell I've just been punched in the gut. The idea that a disease, a terrible drama, is tied to my birth.

My grandmother sometimes said that she gave me her life. It might not have been my life I was living, in the end, but a life borrowed or stolen, hers and my mother's.

My grandmother wanted to save face in the red brick bungalow in Ville Saint-Laurent, surrounded by neigh-bours who peered into the wide living room window looking for silhouettes behind the velvet curtains, nou-veaux suburbanites whose wives had tea together in the afternoon, aspics in the fridge next to the Jell-O pudding. Even if times were changing, gossip still held sway. And because my grandmother's pride was as lofty as her hope of improving her lot in life, she sent my mother away, in exile in Quebec City, to see her brother. Or was it my mother who chose her destination when she was told to leave? Did my mother open the door without wondering where she would go, without thinking she might disappear, maybe forever? Was it my mother who ran away, secretly hoping they would go looking for her, or else telling herself she would never go back? Did she land at her brother's as a temporary solution, until she could find a better option, or, because she couldn't think about the future, did she move there out of desperation, a wanderer, barely present, willing to live an invisible life?

She lived there for a while, several weeks or several months, until the day my brother's wife had had enough of sharing her life with her young sister-in-law. It was decided to move her into an apartment a friend had offered, here and there like a dog you tug around, an object shifted from place to place. I don't know if it was far from my uncle's place, or close by, in case of an emergency. Maybe they had no choice and she was moved into the first place they found. I don't know if my mother was happy there, if she needed solitude or suffered from it. I do know that in that apartment that wasn't hers she was almost raped, despite her belly and because of it, because my presence inside her allowed boys every right, the harm was already done so why not take advantage of it. Teenage mothers were easy girls with nothing more to lose, and they weren't allowed to say no. My uncle's friend threw his weight around and against the body of my future mother. She summoned all her strength, who knows how, and managed to kick him out and keep her belly to herself.

My mother, for whom my presence was a threat. My mother, whom to this day I try to protect.

I don't know what neighbourhood they were living in when my mother arrived, or where she ended up moving when my uncle's wife had had enough. Maybe they found her lying down, her eyes wide open after a night of insomnia, hands crossed over the belly that wouldn't stop growing, and which had already changed everything. Maybe my mother was worried about what would happen to her now that she was an impediment to her brother's happiness, banished by her own mother, forever disappointed, her mother ashamed, bitter, choked by resentment, her mother who would never forgive her. What would happen to her now that she had proof that her father wasn't strong enough to challenge his wife, and that he was abandoning his darling little girl to her fate.

Was my uncle's wife, who didn't want children, afraid that her home would become a nursery, or was she merely stepping back instead of getting wedged between the rock of my grandparents and the hard place my mother found herself in? Maybe she had no sympathy for this young woman, victim of an accident, and actually held it against her not to have been more careful, to have been naive, to have allowed herself to be seduced and not to have known what to do afterward, even though everybody knows, every woman, she didn't want children and even she knew quite well how not to make a baby, and, if the unfortunate should happen, how to get rid of it.

Maybe because she knew all that, because she didn't want kids, the marriage eventually ended, and my grandmother, whose reputation had already taken one on the nose with her teen-mom daughter, hated her prodigal son for having gone from newlywed to divorcé. It was unacceptable. She would have to explain it to her friends and their neighbours, and once more my grandmother would be ashamed. Her children never stopped shaming her, and all the others who grew their hair long, burned their bras, and turned against God.

But my mother stayed a girl. She embodied duality: she was still just a girl, and she was a mother, a mother trapped in the body of a girl.

My mother liked to say that she kept her girlish weight, that after nine months she had gained only the added weight of the tiny baby I was. She said this, and I admired her for having stayed so thin, I envied her body, impervious to change, I respected her will to resist. She had held onto childhood even into motherhood. She had mortgaged her own childhood and would welcome mine more like a sister than a mother. I wasn't always sure which one of us was older.

This is during the October Crisis. My mother's cousin has just been named justice minister, Pierre Elliott Trudeau has imposed the War Measures Act, and over the course of a few days 500 Quebec citizens have been arbitrarily arrested. Questioned in the legislature after the dust has settled, my mother's minister cousin breaks down in tears. Nobody in the family will ever dare talk about that either.

I was born on the wrong side, surrounded by suits rather than bombs, landing in my grandfather's family, a surprising laboratory of doctors, lawyers, and writers. It was a world of elegant and educated boys who left their mark on Quebec history, according to the newspaper clippings my grandmother kept, which she gave me one day, fodder for a genealogy of heroes.

When she met my grandfather, my grandmother had bourgeois aspirations that her future husband's family promised to satisfy. He was elegant in his finest white suit at Old Orchard Beach. But he was also asthmatic and scrawny, sickly, an ugly duckling, a failed businessman. He had studied pharmacy at the Sorbonne between the wars and claimed to have tossed francs at Edith Piaf when she sang under the window of his room in Montmartre. He remembered German planes on display in the streets of Paris, an impressive procession. It was a story he told over and over again.

For health reasons, my grandfather was never a soldier, and he was never able to become a businessman either. He had to close a business immediately after opening it, a drugstore he passed along to one of his brothers because of the pneumonia that kept him bedridden for a long time. To feed the family, my grandmother was forced for a time to work at Grolier. One of her colleagues was the young Réjean Ducharme. The soon-to-be-celebrated novelist and equally famous recluse was a strange boy, my grandmother said, quiet and aloof—a mysterious acquaintance who was much more interesting for her than the isolation of a housewife.

My mother didn't have an abortion and even if she had wanted to I don't know what she would've done, what angel-maker she would have gone to, or if a doctor would have done the deed, a friend of my grandfather's brothers, or our family doctor, willing to purify one of his girls. My grandfather was the youngest in his family. His mother had been hit by the first tramway that ran in Montreal when he was a boy, and his father was a country doctor who wrote farm novels in his spare time. He had already been dead for a long time when my own roots were planted in the womb of my young mother. After I was born, when my mother was alone in Quebec City, my grandfather asked his oldest brother for advice, and he was ordered to take his daughter back and with her his granddaughter, because there I was.

I was born somewhere after the dark years of Duplessis and before Morgentaler, after the Indigenous right to vote, after women had access to the Pill.

In 1967, Lester B. Pearson established the Royal Commission on the Status of Women. Six months later, divorce was legalized in Canada. But Pope Paul VI condemned the use of oral contraceptives, and no one explained to my mother how to avoid making babies.

I don't know what happened, if some protective membrane was laid between skin and skin before their bodies came together, if the question came up or if nothing was said, if silence was golden because, in any case, it was up to her to take care of it. What I do know is that my life is the result of ignorance or innocence, nonchalance or a misunderstanding: a mistake and an accident.

I can't imagine my ultra-religious grandmother insisting that her daughter terminate a pregnancy, and yet, without a doubt, she did. Her shame was stronger than her love of God and what good is it to love God in the eyes of everyone to keep up appearances when your own daughter is thumbing her nose at you with her belly full of sin?

In 1968, Henry Morgentaler opened an abortion clinic. By the time I was born, the month of May, and with it the unrest in France and elsewhere, was over. The rebellious season had come and gone.

My mother could have found a way to get rid of me, but she always said it never even crossed her mind, her voice full of the assurance of someone who is telling the whole truth and nothing but the truth, as if to convince me that I was wanted, when she didn't have to convince me, since I was there before her to prove it, and repeating the words insistently implied that, on the contrary, it had crossed her mind, and the mind of everyone around her, that there had been pressure, that simply getting rid of the pregnancy would have been the best solution for everyone, for her mother, her father, her brother, for her, for the man who did not become my father, and even maybe—who knows—for me too.

There are no photos of my mother pregnant with me, no proof of the existence of that distraught, desperate young woman, the young woman who doubted whether she should have me or not.

I've never thanked her for giving me life. I've always felt that it didn't concern me, since it wasn't a choice I made. We don't choose to be born, and we have to make do with life, or else make the terrible choice to end it, to free the self from what is always considered a gift, something bestowed.

Like most teenagers, I wanted to yell that I hadn't asked to be born. I never did, I bit back the words, buried and swallowed, and although the thought sometimes surfaces, it's only when I've lost track of what my life means, the way you can lose your bearings and all at once not know where you are or where to head. During those strange moments when I find myself outside of myself, twinned, and I see myself as others might see me, I live in my body as if I were not there, as if I were not me.

I don't know what meant so much to my mother, the child she imagined, the ruins of a love affair, a last-ditch attempt to bring back the man she wanted, or if she was looking for freedom, an accelerated adulthood that would take her far from her tough-love mother, that woman who could reject with one hand and stifle with the other, whom my mother had come to fear when she was still small, wan and frail, an overprotected, sickly child, a child loved and hated by the headstrong woman who kept the books and who regretted more than anything not having had the chance to study, a woman who might have spent her life travelling, curious and hungry for beauty, and instead found herself trapped between four walls, forced to look after a fragile little girl who had emerged from her body and who, when they found themselves alone together, would immediately begin to cry.

My mother's mother was a woman nothing could fulfill or appease, except, perhaps for an instant, jewellery, furs, Limoges, and maybe my grandfather's patience as he stretched out to kiss her cheek or her neck, to soothe away a misunderstanding or a bad mood. Then my grandmother would drop her eyes and a little smile played on her lips. They were still in love.

My grandfather was already old when I was born. He was a retired civil servant, a golfer, television watcher. He would lay me on his chest to nap and the two of us would sleep on the front seat of the Cadillac parked in the driveway of the house on Rochon Street.

My grandparents' house was one of the first built in the new development. They saw so many other houses spring up and with them neighbours and Saturday afternoon drinks in chairs woven with wide synthetic bands, sitting in a circle in the grass, a plastic spear through an olive or a maraschino cherry leaning in each glass. My grandfather called every squirrel that nested in their tree George. I can still see him kneeling down, a peanut in one outstretched hand and in the other a cigar.

Later—I am thirty—he is hunched, shaky, weak, incontinent. I travel across the city rain or shine to spend the evening with him so he won't be alone and so my grandmother, who's younger than he is, can visit her group of ladies, go out to the movies, play bridge. I make supper, I help him to bed after having given him the pill that eases the anxiety night brings, and I stay and watch TV in the next room, listening. I check on him while he sleeps, watching his chest rise and fall to make sure he's still there, with me.

My grandfather wasn't like my grandmother, he didn't fight against death. He fought to slide toward death, for release.

One night he fell into a deep sleep and never woke up. The nurses still came to his room to shake him, to call him, to see if he could be roused. Once or twice he blinked an eye open before falling back asleep, once or twice, then never again.

My grandfather wanted to die. The time had come. What was left of life wasn't worth living anymore—the thin gums, wobbly legs, the humiliation of being diapered. He said one word before sinking, only one: his nickname for me when the two of us were alone, a name meant just for him and me, which he never used in front of others, his eyes full of the tenderness that tells us who we belong to and what love means.

One night, we're sitting together at the small kitchen table. I've made tea after dinner. I interrogate him softly, bruising open his memory to see what he remembers, to find out if the little I know is really true—my uncle, the banishment to Quebec, the anger and the threats, the broken hearts. My grandfather's memory is going. He can remember every detail of his childhood, the antics between Saint-Hilaire and Beloeil, firecrackers, the frights he gave his mother, and how from the age of eight he would drive his father's cart in the middle of the night to take him to patients in labour. He can describe the beginning of time, but he forgets what just happened. So when he answers my questions I don't really know whether he really remembers or if he's making things up, if the past is coming back to him or if he's imagining it based on the present, based on what he knows now or on what he wishes. Even if he seems to remember, I'm not sure, and I tell myself that in the end there is no more truth in what really happened than in what was wished, thought, or dreamed.

I don't remember what I said, if I asked him what it was like the day they came back for us, my mother somewhere in Quebec and me at the orphanage. I don't remember how I broached the question of my almost-adoption, but he went quiet for a moment, his grey eyes an enigma. Then he answered, without any hesitation, There was never any question about it. You were always part of this family.

I'll never know if he remembered right or if he was giving me a whitewashed version of the past, if he was telling me now what he had thought and felt at the time and kept to himself, or shared but no one listened, or if he was telling the story as he would have liked it to happen because I was here now and we loved each other very much, we were tied to each other by a length of invisible string, our complicity woven in silence and gesture.

His words were a quiet truth that had always bound us to each other, the words of the man who had decided to come get us shortly before Christmas in the middle of a blizzard, the storm everywhere, outside and inside as well, inside him, between my grandmother and him, my grandmother and her daughter, my uncle and his young wife, my uncle and his parents, between my mother and all these people and the whole world suddenly become strange to her. A fleeting, mysterious storm, one I lived as an infant, intimate and inscrutable, the nameless pain of a tiny being who might have been abandoned, and for whom time cannot be traced. And then shame, forever, because that baby had been a thing, disposable, and later a thing reclaimed.

People like to say it doesn't leave a mark, we don't remember anything, a baby's memory is a dark screen. The specific memory might be forgotten, but the story exists and the body, mysteriously, remembers.

I don't know how my mother lived during the days, weeks, months before giving birth, between when she found out she was pregnant and the moment I was born, between meeting the man who would not become my father and the moment at which she realized she had become my mother, between being put to sleep and waking up with a brand-new baby next to her, between the moment she left me in the arms of a nun at the orphanage and when she came to get me, between giving me life and abandoning me. That story I know nothing about, almost nothing, it's a story full of holes, like a loosely knitted blanket, it's an uncertain story, a story with no story, a crossword puzzle without clues.

I imagine that my mother took the news of my birth like a blackout. Life stopped, the ground opened up beneath her, she thought she would die or go crazy, she tried to wake up from the nightmare and shuck off her own skin, become someone else, close her eyes, start all over again.

What else does a young, twenty-year-old woman think about in 1968, when the world really might be changing. She's from a too-good-to-be-true family, pious, religious, parents who want the best for their daughter—a private girls' school and later a well-to-do husband. What does a young girl think about when she's never seen anything but a suburban bungalow living room and a school desk or church pew, except maybe an occasional ski trip, bowling alley, a movie house, a walk along the river?

It's spring, she has other things on her mind than social upheaval, rebellion, and the winds of change. It's happening inside her, my rebellious mother punished for a bit of stolen freedom, divine retribution like in those stories about birds or locusts unleashed on earth by a livid God, or a relentless storm that stops time by cloaking the world in thick white. I imagine her astonishment, her disbelief. She's paralyzed, which is nothing compared to her parents' fury, her mother's rage, the disappointment on her father's face, because a pregnant belly is so obvious, it speaks volumes about what the kids are fighting for, and what is forbidden to her. It could have been ten years earlier, twenty, when orphanages were a nightmare of children to sell or give away, and those who stayed were taken advantage of at night in the dormitories or smacked around in a dark corner at the end of the hall, their files doctored for money, mental-health diagnoses, land sacrificed for the good of the religious communities in bed with the state, the darkness of a meek nation that refused to grow up.

I tell myself that at that moment my mother lost sight of the horizon, of the image of the woman she would become. I tell myself she lost her breath; a bunch of scenes had just been brutally cut from the film of her life. My mother never fully recovered from that rift, that ellipsis, she never really got over it. Her excision from the world, that banishment, followed her all her life.

She called him after I was born.

I don't know whether she called from Montreal or Quebec, from the hospital or after having left me at the orphanage, or after having gotten me back. I don't know if my future depended on his reply, if what he said after she told him that he had a daughter—he was thinking about her, he was leaving the country—if those words changed the course of my life. What would I have become if he had changed his mind, if he had been languishing, waiting, just a little desperate, for my mother's phone call, having lost track of her because nobody wanted to tell him where she had gone, if he had regretted his cavalier dismissal, his suggestion that carrying a child was a cliché. If he had regretted his scorn when she refused to leave him alone while others before her had suffered in silence, dealing alone with the result of their passion? What would my life be like today if upon reflection he had instead come around and decided to take things in hand, to claim the child, to be her father?

But that's not how the story goes, and when the priest back in Montreal sprinkles water on my head, I am given my mother's name.

In the photo I am swaddled in white. It's winter, and I'm in the arms of my aunt, the one who wanted my mother to go flaunt her belly elsewhere. My aunt is smiling and next to her my grandmother faces away with her fur coat and her large hat. Her brother is celebrating the baptism, the good Father my great-uncle, who lives in the presbytery, where the whole family is invited to ring in the new year. Everyone except the new mother and her baby. And on New Year's Day, for a few hours, everyone pretends nothing happened, that a young girl didn't get pregnant out of wedlock, the father didn't take off, that she didn't decide to keep her baby.

No one's ever really told me those stories, they're just ready-made sentences, words glued together into a sequence until the finale of rejection, without telling the story of what actually happened. Nothing about what was said to exclude mother and child, nothing about the weather, the clothes they wore, the tone of voice, the shouts and sighs, fists shaken, arms raised to the heavens, backs turned. Nothing about what was left once everyone had gone, nothing about what traces of her banishment remained once she was returned to grace. Nothing about abandoning a young mother and her newborn daughter because it's unthinkable to invite them to celebrate the new year in a presbytery. Nothing about the bodies heading out into the night, relieved to be able to forget their shame for a while.

When my mother and her brother die, I will lose even the memory of that amnesia. I won't even be able to remember the fact that I don't remember anything because I was never told anything, no one ever recorded the first instants of my life. I made up my own story bit by bit and I'll have to unfold it and stitch it together from pieces of the past. For the first time, I dive in, I can't think about anything else. Don't you have anything happier to write about, my mother would say if I told her what I'm doing, she wouldn't quite understand why I'm telling that story again. Nor would my grandmother, if she were still with us. She would just wave the conversation away, as she did if I ever dared ask her a question: I ought to forget all that, there was no point in revisiting it. She would shake her head wordlessly, drop a curtain of ice between us to make it very clear that she holds it against me that I am writing what I am writing, not only this but also everything I've written since she's been gone, and even the life I've lived, the affairs I've had that she wouldn't understand, and the struggles, it's better not to struggle and you shouldn't go up against anyone, bosses, colleagues, the state. Anger is a private thing, you shouldn't risk alienating anyone or losing your job. Don't change the world because the world is fine and if you simply must start something, choose the calmest path and the straightest.

I move forward, absorbed by the reel of invisible photographs, a film only I can see. My story is an invented story, not only because I don't know it, but because I can't fathom it, as if imagination itself had been lost, it's been banned in the theatre of silence I'm locked in, me, the little girl without a story, the child it was better not to mention, tabula rasa, delete the whole world by scratching out this blonde child with pale skin, laughing and lively on her tricycle, her short curls pulled on top of her head with a ribbon, a spatula in her hand in front of a birthday cake covered in writing, having an imaginary phone conversation in footed pyjamas, sitting on a wooden bench in the first row of her class photo, refusing to smile over her braces.

Fade out. I'm flipping between my story and the plot of a TV series I'm hooked on. I binge-watch, not so much to forget my own life, but to be able to think.

This time, I'm in Seattle, behind a sheet of rain, a curtain of tears, next to a redheaded detective with translucent skin, her face naked, open, guileless. The detective has been investigating the murder of a young girl found folded in a bag in the trunk of a car at the bottom of a lake. The bag is full of water, the girl's wrists are cut up, the investigation is going round in circles. There are no witnesses, the suspects arrive at the scene of the crime, so many false leads and the body of the young girl continues to sleep at the crossroads. We find out that the detective was abandoned by her mother when she was small, that she grew up in foster homes, that she has a child herself now, a little boy she loves more than anything even though she's not a very good mother, she leaves him alone in the middle of the night, feeds him frozen dinners, tucks him into a motel room, sometimes puts him in danger because the investigation matters more than anything. She can't help coming back to this murder, to the young victim's bedroom, the crime she has to solve.

The story is that the young girl who disappeared wasn't the daughter of the man who raised her. Shortly before her death, she found an old shoebox that belonged to her mother, full of pictures, objects, and letters. A letter her mother had written to the man who'd gotten her pregnant, telling him he was going to be a father. There's an address, but the envelope was never mailed.

Eighteen years later, the young girl rings a doorbell, and a man opens the door. He invites her to sit down, makes tea, listens to her speak, she's unhappy, suffering, she says she wants to leave, leave the city, this life, live somewhere else. She asks him questions, what her mother was like when they met. She asks him whether they were in love, and he says yes. He describes a happy young woman, curious, rebellious, a woman the young girl has a hard time seeing in the woman she knows, the mother whose face is drawn too tight, the woman she's about to leave behind. She's brought a backpack and has made up her mind to leave Seattle that night, leave her room in the family home, and leave behind a story too heavy to carry. She will go after having met for the first time the man who was never a father to her and maybe making her peace with him, and she might have started over somewhere else if she hadn't fallen into the hands of another man, a random stranger, her killer.

Near the Jeffery Hale Hospital, in 1968, on Sainte-Foy Road, there is the Saint-Vincent de Paul, a home run by nuns for young mothers and the children they are still often forced to abandon. Was that where my mother left me? Was that where she handed me over, telling the sister she was absolutely not to give me to anyone else, she was only leaving me there temporarily, long enough to get her act together, she would come back to get me and take me with her and start over, please, I promise, I swear.

I find an old archival photo of the orphanage on the Web, from the thirties. In the picture, nurses are pushing carriages full of children.

They say that between 1950 and 1970, thousands of children in Quebec were sent to live with rich families because the orphanages were overcrowded. The children would first be placed in Quebec, then elsewhere in Canada, and, when there were no families left to take them, overseas.

What would have happened if someone had taken me, if by mistake or out of greed some nun decided to give me up for adoption or sell me to a rich American couple who wanted a white baby? I might have grown up in Alabama or Nebraska, I'd be looking for my mother, a young French Canadian with no connection to the backwoods of the United States, and I would speak English, or I would have grown up on a ranch, surrounded by potato fields in Idaho or in the middle of the Colorado mountains, in a chic Fifth Avenue building in New York City or near Chinatown in San Francisco, and maybe I would have been told nothing, my life tumbling on quietly, my days with no sharp edges, or they would have told me what they knew, and under those circumstances, the existence of my father, my real father, wouldn't matter.

Orphanages closed their doors in 1972 on the tail of the peace and love comet, between the October Crisis and the feminist revolution. It was a close call: if I had been born four years later, there would have been no orphanage to drop off babies in cradles. A few years earlier and I might've been a Duplessis orphan.

The orphanages were overflowing with sin. A procuress might approach a pregnant girl in a restaurant and offer to pay her costs in exchange for the child, a child purchased by Jews who wanted to be parents but couldn't adopt a Catholic child through the orphanages, since the nuns stood by their own God. The girl gave birth in a makeshift baby factory on the Plateau, a rooming house where newborns were sold for up to ten thousand dollars.

But it was 1968 and I was not adopted. My mother came back after a few days, a week at most, with her parents. I was never really abandoned.

I've never let myself imagine what my mother went through. It is as unfathomable to me as what I myself might have felt as a little baby, and which maybe surfaces now and again in spite of me—the fear of disappearing, of being forgotten for good.

Either I never really found the words, or I lacked the courage to say them. To speak of certain things is to give them the power to exist. I understood very early on that breaking my silence would be treason. Treason can't even be avoided by writing, because writing is even worse.

The Saint-Vincent de Paul played a major role in teaching medicine and pediatrics. In 1929, the massive influx of new children heralded its golden age. For the nuns, looking after the newborns, who were housed on the second floor, was a monumental task. There were so many children that, to keep track of them, everyone in a dormitory was given the same last name.

I don't know if I had a name during those days I spent in the orphanage, if someone chose one or if I already had the name that is mine today. I don't even know if I was renamed before my great-uncle the priest did the official deed, or what number I was assigned to identify me among all those cradles. Maybe for a time I bore the family name of a big room full of babies and for a few days I was called something like Tremblay.

I tell myself that they must have listened to my mother, they must have taken her at her word and I was accepted as a temporary orphan, denied my mother's arms but not anonymous like the other babies were, those who had lost both parents, dead or disappeared, mothers and fathers known or unknown who had also lost the child they loved, parents from whom a child was torn, or given up against their will.

There is a pure dignity to being an orphan, probably because of that parental longing, a desire felt and repressed or dismissed, lives ripped from each other. Orphans make us cry because orphans are children deprived first and foremost of their mother. Others, who are missing only a father, the illegitimate children born out of wedlock, so-called natural children, the children of sin or love, are bastards. The accidental is in their blood. They share that shameful pregnancy and birth with their mother, because they weren't wanted. They are unworthy because they were not sanctioned before the altar. Their arrival in the world is to be hidden rather than celebrated.

Bastard. The word that must not be spoken. The word that shatters silence. It's what the little girl across the way spat at me one day, like a ball thrown too hard for me to catch. Goddamn bastard. A vulgar word, a swear word, used whenever, for no reason. Each time I hear it I can't breathe.

You're a bastard like you're a son of a bitch. There's no such thing as just a bastard child: the mother is a bastard too, she is an accidental mother, a half-mother, a failure.

What I know is what I've seen dozens of times in movies, an image that grabs me as if it were mine, something about me or that belongs to me: a shot of an enormous room with dozens of metal cribs lined up side by side. Dressed in white, nuns zigzag between the rows of beds, bending over the bars, extending a hand toward a swaddled baby. They look like brides. Their day begins at seven o'clock in the morning at the foot of the altar and then they go tend to the little ones, *those pure images of the Christchild who see as trespass against Him what is done to the least of them*. Each one has a clearly defined role—wash, diaper, clothe, feed, walk. The machine is well oiled.

What I also know is that the nuns used a dumbwaiter to bring the babies left at the door up to their floor. Sometimes a note was pinned to the blanket, some detail for their care, the given name.

I took bottles in the arms of women who were not my mother, women whose blessed wombs would likely never bear children. They bathed me and swaddled me, they laid me in a crib, maybe they rocked me and hummed nursery rhymes, kissed me on the forehead, maybe they were tender and maybe not, maybe their gestures were mechanical, distracted, maybe even brutal, because how is it possible to love so many babies at once?

A lifetime later, I unfold the memory. I look at it from far away at first and I bring it closer slowly, little by little, worried and uncertain. For a long time I am stock-still, fearful before the secret projected up on the screen.

I was pale and freckled with blonde hair that turned red, darker and darker, like copper, so that I was sometimes asked where I was from, the Netherlands or from Ireland, which made me blush.

When I was eight, nine, or ten, I was a tomboy. That was the fashion, we wore button-down shirts over turtlenecks and bellbottom Wranglers. The freedom of not having to belong to one side or another. Pictures from that time show a glimpse of crooked teeth hidden behind a forced smile, a scrawny body, a flat chest. Being a girl didn't mean much of anything back then. It still doesn't mean much to me.

All my life since childhood I've been told by strangers that I look just like someone they know, a friend, cousin, acquaintance, it's uncanny how much you look like her. I've come to imagine a large family scattered around the world, a paper chain of others like me, all fathered by the same man, a single face hewn by his hand.

My grandmother, to avoid telling me she didn't find me pretty, would say, You're a smart one.

For a long time I believed my father was dead and no one had told me. No one can tell me if he's alive. His death was a childhood fantasy, a way not to wait for him anymore. But as time goes by, his death becomes a hypothesis that reality is likely to confirm. The more years pass, the more I put him to death in my head.

For a long time I waited for witnesses. I hoped for a voice from the past, someone who would have seen everything, heard everything, and who could tell me the whole truth. I got some documents. I parsed every line. It didn't change anything, there was nothing to discover. What was taken away cannot be brought back.

I can't invent stories because the story I carry is a story I'm constantly reinventing, it absorbs me and inhabits me because I have no control over it and what I don't know takes up all the room. It looks a lot like the relentless sorrow that doesn't let go, that won't let go of anything, when someone dies and you can't touch, hold, or feel the body of the beloved any longer, you don't have access to it anymore, the arms remember but when they reach out they gather only air.

What I know. Quebec, December 1968, the nurse fills out a declaration of birth. She writes in the name of the mother, then asks the father's name. The mother answers that there is nothing to write. The nurse, horrified, protests, *Madame*! Your daughter must have a father!

What I know. Montreal, November 2013, a nurse fills out a medical chart.

"Are there any diseases in your family? Cancer, diabetes, heart disease?"

"No."

"On your mother's side?"

"Nothing."

"Your father's?"

"I have no idea. I don't know anything about my father."

"I'm sorry."

When I pore over a map of Quebec City, I don't understand anything. I can't make sense of it, I lose my bearings, I mix everything up.

Quebec is a city I know without knowing it, a familiar place that always seems foreign, a mirror that doesn't show my reflection. Quebec is a city I arrive in each time for the first time and only ever see the surface, sliding along it as over the portrait of someone I don't know. If I had to love Quebec City, it would be for its fortress walls, the affliction of its escarpments, the phantom battles that rage on across its plains.

Quebec is a white city. Maybe because I was born in December.

I dig around in the archives of the Sisters of Charity. On November 20, 1944, a newspaper announces that Quebec Airways Company transported twenty-six babies from Quebec City to Chicoutimi, where there were a lot of adoptions requests. I don't see the year of my birth listed anywhere in the documents I flip through. There's a gap between 1950 and 1972, the year the orphanage was closed, as if 1968 has been crossed out.

On Radio-Canada, January 27, 1970, the journalist Michelle Tisseyre interviews a woman. The story goes back a few years. The woman's face is hidden from the camera. Her body could be anyone's. Only her voice, flat, sad, empty, her sensible square haircut, and before her the journalist, patient, who asks her questions delicately and leaves room for silence, to let the tears flow, without judgment.

She is the daughter of strict, religious parents, a provincial girl who was never told anything about how babies are made. She falls in love with a man who is fully aware of how naive she is and shortly after they meet she finds out she is carrying a child. The man suggests an abortion, the young woman refuses. She leaves the countryside and flees to the big city, gives birth at the Hôpital de la Miséricorde, leaves her child at the orphanage while she works to reimburse the hospital for what she owes for her stay during her pregnancy and the birth. When it's time to leave, when her time has run out, she doesn't have enough money to pay, and she is forced to abandon the baby.

This happens at a time when orphanages in Quebec are being converted into psychiatric institutions and reform schools, before the state has taken it upon itself to replace absent fathers by giving single mothers the means to keep their children.

The orphanages are called Mercy, Deliverance, Providence, Charity.

They are called orphanage, school, institution, kindergarten, receiving depot, children's home, foundling home, foster home, centre, house of refuge.

Are you obsessed, the journalist asks softly, Is this something that haunts you? Yes, the woman replies, I think about it every day.

I've often been told that it's better to have no father at all than to have a good-for-nothing for a father.

I heard it from a friend who was abused by her bipolar father, who required that every single door in the house, including the bathroom door, be kept open.

I heard it from an older woman, raised by an alcoholic, whose mother would go retrieve him at the pub, dead drunk on the corner of the bar, and haul him home, where he would collapse again on the kitchen table.

I heard it from a young girl, who got punched in the face every time she said the wrong thing.

How many times have I heard these stories, about how disappointing fathers can be, about how fathers are absent even when they're present, and present when we'd rather they weren't? I'm trapped between wanting and truth—wanting something to be made real out of so much silence and mystery, and the truth that says that being a father, a real father, doesn't have much to do with genetics.

All my life, without doing it on purpose, I have surrounded myself with bastards and discards, and, probably to try to set something right, I have loved them intensely.

I've lost count of the girlfriends whose fathers were dead-beats or losers, violent men, cruel men, indecent men, and they didn't get how I could miss that. I had to explain that it wasn't so much that the father was missing, but the story about him, unknown.

I sometimes get the feeling that the image has faded, my desire is waning. Time is hollowing itself out and the invented figure of a fictional father falls away and slowly disappears.

Maybe he's always been dead, and time has nothing to do with it? Maybe he passed away shortly after I was born, in an accident or from a horrible illness, maybe he committed a crime and was put in jail, or he became a monk and is hiding somewhere in Nepal. Maybe he never really did anything with his life, or maybe he decided to end it.

I don't know, and because I don't know, I catch myself thinking that one day he'll reappear. There's no mourning because there has been no death. There are only too many words, and not enough.

A few days after my grandmother's death, sorting through her papers, looking for her birth certificate, we learn that she was born forty-eight hours before her parents were married. She was the baby, so she and those who came before her, all the other children, were illegitimate. Joseph and Albertine weren't married.

I reread the words, incredulous and delighted. With my mother's pregnancy, I tell myself, shame caught up to my grandmother, as if she had been cursed or fallen victim to some atavism that even her marriage to my grandfather, the youngest in a family of notaries and doctors, rich and educated, had been unable to erase.

Once, in my last moments at her bedside, my computer on my lap, my grandmother snapped out of her sleep for a second. That was the Cheyne-Stokes breathing showing itself: she slept most of the time, her body wanting oxygen, her heart exhausted, but that day, seeing me at the foot of her bed, my fingers on the keyboard, she asked if I was working on my new novel.

A few months before her death, I helped my grandmother get ready for a party. She wasn't sure she wanted to go out, but I insisted. I helped her dress, doing up the tiny buttons her fingers couldn't handle and closing the clasp on the string of pearls she wanted to wear. At the door, I told her to call me when she got home to tell me everything. She kissed me and said, You are like a mother to me.

Another time, during the last hours of her life, she suddenly opened her eyes, caught me looking at her, and asked, Are you studying my face?

She was dying, there was nothing more to be done. I could see it in the doctor's eyes, a sadness when I described my grandmother holding her breath and he explained what it meant, my grandmother was dying. Afterward, she stared at me with the question in her eyes, wanting to know. I didn't have the courage to say it, so she did: This will be the room of death.

My grandmother was a secretive woman. She acted like she had forgotten everything, but really she had closed her past life away. We knew almost nothing of her childhood, her youth. We didn't know exactly how many brothers and sisters she had, we didn't know where she came from, and we especially didn't know what was so terrible that she so clearly refused to talk about it. It was as if by marrying she had traded her story for my grand-father's.

At the end of her life, she confided that her father had been a heavy drinker. Her mother had finally left him, taking all the children with her. When I asked my grandmother whether her father had been violent, she answered, No, but he wasn't a nice man.

My grandmother had brothers no one had ever met. We suspected some fuss about inheritance, a family torn apart by greed, bitterness, regret, money. We assumed that the boys and the girls had gone their separate ways. My grandmother's older sisters had sacrificed their young lives to take care of their mother. After her mother's death, my grandmother hadn't been able to get away from them, even after she married. Simone and Jeanne were there to stay, much to the despair of my grandfather who, when he fell in love with this tall, beautiful woman, didn't realized that instead of one he would be getting three.

The two sisters-in-law ruled the roost. After her last sister died, my grandmother, her head down and her voice filled with tears, told me, Now I'm really an orphan.

One day, Simone was lecturing my mother, her goddaughter. She was not to get married, she warned, so she could devote herself to my aging grandmother.

I don't know if Simone told my mother that before or during her pregnancy, or even after. I don't know if my presence in the world was a way for my mother to escape her fate.

I don't know how closely kept my mother was, if they tried to keep her at home, forbade her from going out, if, on the night they met, her parents had set a curfew, if they waited for her to come home before going to bed, if they were suspicious, if they thought she had changed, if they guessed there was something going on, if they felt it.

It wasn't the first time, he wasn't the first boy, but, although she didn't know it yet, he was the one she would take the plunge with, stand up to her mother, pull away from her father, show them that the weak, breathless little girl wasn't all nice and no naughty. Beneath the anxiety and shyness thrummed heat lightning. She wanted to be the one to seduce, she could let herself be carried away too. And he was the one waiting at the other end, that tall blond man with whom she would play at freedom. The man who would become not my father.

I imagine my mother in the house in Ville Saint-Laurent. She's getting ready to go out. I can hear my grandmother doing the dishes, her face closed up, her disapproving sighs growing deeper as she clatters the cutlery. She stacks the plates noisily, opens and closes the cupboards without catching them to stop the slam, while my grandfather pretends he hears nothing, reading the newspaper on the sofa. My grandmother wants to keep her daughter to herself, even if that daughter prevents her from living her life, even if she embodies everything that's expected of my grandmother and which she cannot stand, even if she begrudges her the hours spent taking care of her. My grandfather tells her when she has to be home, perhaps a little roughly. He avoids looking at her, to make her feel good and guilty, and to sidestep my grandmother's anger. Maybe he has nothing against his daughter going out for the evening, or maybe it annoys him, he disagrees but he chooses to say nothing. Maybe he's already scolded her, but it's no use repeating it, he knows when to stop.

I don't know if my mother went out with friends that night, or if she already had a date with him. I don't know how she crossed the city, by bus or by car, if someone came to pick her up, or if she met her friends at the coffee shop. I wonder if she drank and if she danced.

I imagine the scene when they saw each other for the first time. I tell myself he saw her and crossed the room to meet her. I do not tell myself they met through a common friend who introduced them. In my movie it's love at first sight, a dance, star-crossed lovers, and I tell myself that my whole life hangs in that opening sequence.

My life is a detective novel without a murder, without detectives and without victims, a film poorly cast and badly edited, a story with no beginning and no end. This isn't a childhood tale, it's the story of what's missing.

I dream of reinventing myself, exchanging my imagined life for someone else's instead of living like a hostage to my blackout memory, revisiting the story told forever, the mythology that's become the old slipper of my inner life and which I trudge around in by cowardice or laziness, wanting to feel nothing. It is the thing I serve up to those who love me when in fact I am ashamed, I feel like I've betrayed them.

I write as if I'm haunted by a case to solve, my mind is under siege, my gaze is set on an invisible horizon. I exhaust myself with unlikely situations and impossible calculations. I dream of showing up at the police station asking to see the file. They'll set a folder before me and I will turn the pages, taking note of places and dates, memorizing the names on every line, I will follow the investigation step by step, the transcripts, photographs, confessions, accusations. I'd like to see how it unfolds, one blank space after another, the gaps filled in like those pictures in colouring books that appear as kids connect the dots, each one in a fixed order, numbered, and how the image is complete, the line closed, with relief, no doubt, the satisfaction of a job well done, case closed, how we arrive safely, how we satisfy a craving.

But there is no file, only bits of paper that fly up when I try to put them in a folder. There is no file, and I don't know what the crime was anymore. I'm writing to try to rewind. I watch each sequence over and over again, I listen to the soundtrack again, I search for clues. Nothing fits, but it's the investigation that matters, not solving the mystery, but the path to get there.

I've reached the end of my TV series. They found the culprit, the mystery is solved. But the body count has been climbing. The investigation into the murder of the young girl found in the trunk of the car at the bottom of the lake led to other deaths, murders, suicides, a chain of interrupted lives. When her partner triumphantly congratulates the detective, she answers, her eyes filled with tears, Really? Tell me, what did we find?

Sometimes I feel a kind of tenderness, the sweep of a caress, for the words I'm writing, words that are at once the mother and the child to whom she's given birth.

I don't caress the father. I wouldn't know how or why. It's less anger than spite. I give up, faced with the only thing that's true: he's not here. Besides, I don't know about ghosts, only how to clothe them in wind and words.

I write idly, like a sleepwalker. I don't know if I'm dreaming, and I don't know if I'm making things up. I wander from one window to another, I jump through time, I progress blindly, keeping a bit of distance from the stories I tell, afraid to be swallowed or washed away. I don't know what awaits me along this road, or when I will get to the end. I've never gone all the way to the end.

I write automatically, I drop sentences and my body absorbs the shock, my body is abandoning me, it can't go on, my back is knotted up, burning, my muscles are sore, my fingers freezing and numb.

I write, little by little, language exhausted by a secret, unnameable punishment, a dictionary I wish I could escape from, exile myself from the country of suffering. Jump overboard.

I'm writing this book slowly, as if it were my last chance. As if after this I will have to be silent forever.

The room where it all began, the first room, is the hospital room in Quebec's Lower Town. The room after the contractions, the hallway of shame, the forced sleep, the room after the words of a nurse to the young woman twisting in pain before her, My dear, you haven't seen anything yet! That's the room where my mother saw me for the first time when she woke up, and maybe her brother too, or else maybe in the nursery? How many times has he told the story of how, during those days when I wasn't with my mother, when I still don't know where she was, he drove to Montreal and back in the middle of a snowstorm to barge in at his parents' and declare that if anyone would be adopting that baby, it would be him. I don't know what my uncle threatened, the words he chose. Perhaps he said, If my sister puts the child up for adoption, I will adopt her? Or, If you don't want the child, I will take her? I don't know if he said he would disappear too, keep the baby and leave his parents behind, and if that's how he managed to undermine his father's authority. I don't know what my uncle's wife thought of all this, if he was willing to sacrifice her too to adopt the abandoned child. If he had, what would my mother have said? What would have happened? Would he have taken me with him in order to eventually give me back to her, or would he have kept me to himself? Would he have chosen me for a moment only, or forever? Which family would I have grown up in? Would I have been raised by a brother and sister become parents of a little girl bastard?

What I know. He made the trip, and shortly thereafter, my grandparents followed.

Either I would be abandoned by everyone, or else they would keep me and I would grow up in a family that only half-heartedly wanted me. In either case, I was adopted, sort of chosen, or, put another way, *imported*. That was the word my grandparents used to talk about people who came to settle here, the word likely applied to my father, the man from somewhere else.

I might be an immigrant's daughter. I am an inside-out exile.

There's a link between the orphanage, the little cots wheeled around by a nun dressed in white wearing a wedding veil on her head, those interchangeable ghostly mothers, and my character, the comatose woman in a hospital room, the beautiful, unresponsive face of a woman deeply asleep. There's a link between the hundreds, the thousands of swaddled newborns left in the care of strangers and forced to wait patiently for their turn in a crib, and that woman who haunted me for months, beaten and fallen, sent into sleep, the woman hovering in limbo, the woman who fell like my mother when she was still young, like so many other young women who got pregnant more or less by magic, since even conceiving of their own desire was unfathomable, pregnancies happened to girls without them doing anything, especially not trying to experience pleasure, because in the end it had nothing to do with them, unconscious, fainting with fear, surprised in their sleep, and now they had to be hidden away to save some semblance of honour.

That motionless woman was my mother, pregnant in spite of herself, my mother in exile, waiting for me. She was me, child born of a mystery, forever waiting for my mother and my story.

That sleeping beauty was my mother as I had carried her in my mind, a young woman who fell prey to a curse and who was waiting to be awakened, called out of exile and brought back to herself.

Between 1870 and 1996, in Canada, one hundred and fifty thousand First Nations, Inuit, and Métis children were taken from their parents, snatched from their communities, and deported to one hundred and thirty church-run orphanages. They had to learn a new language and another religion, and forget their family and their community. The idea was to *take the Indian out of the child*. As Duncan Campbell Scott said in 1920, they had to be *absorbed*.

No one in charge ever testified. They were swept under the rug, those children, who were underfed, who were used as guinea pigs in nutritional experiments. Abused, battered, and raped, those children were ignored. We turned a blind eye to thousands of sterilized girls and women. For a long time, no one would name this silent genocide. And in the hope of being able to, despite so many lies and secrets, now we're reaching for reconciliation.

In 2014, in Galway, Ireland, a mass grave was discovered. The bodies of eight hundred babies had been buried between 1925 and 1961 in a septic pit near a home for single mothers. At the time, prostitutes, orphans, the mentally handicapped, girls who had been raped, and girls who were considered easy or too pretty were all locked up in the Magdalene laundries, where they were forced to work as laundresses. The laundries were named after Mary Magdalene, and girls of ill repute were sent there to be rehabilitated and punished. They were turned into slaves in work camps. They were young mothers whose children had been taken away and who had been sent away from their families, prisoners forced into silence behind eternally locked doors, women beaten, humiliated, broken. Locked up immediately after giving birth, their milk coming in and burning up with mastitis, they could say nothing, they couldn't even moan or else they were punished. They were forced to wash sheets, tablecloths, and towels for the hospitals and the big hotels, scrubbing to wash away their guilt, cleanse their souls, pay for their sins.

The rate of infant mortality was extremely high; babies died of hunger and neglect, of childhood diseases, tuberculosis, gastroenteritis, pneumonia. Children went to school with hollow cheeks and swollen bellies. They were made fun of by those who grew up in normal families and who, for a laugh, gave them rocks wrapped in shiny paper, pretending they were candy.

In 1970, the Quebec Civil Code recognized some of the rights of children born out of wedlock, thereby asserting the legal equality of all children regardless of the circumstances of their birth.

In 1981, notions of legitimacy and illegitimacy were officially abolished.

We found a family photo among my grandmother's things, after we had cleaned everything out. All the women are there, my grandmother and her sisters, the two exhausting old aunts, my uncle's wife, and the woman, so young, who will become my mother. Standing behind them, their men, my grandmother's brother the priest, my grandfather, one of his brothers, and my mother's brother, the cherished oldest son. In the picture, only my mother isn't looking at the camera. Her head tilted slightly to the side, she looks like she's smiling, happy and impish, looking off-camera toward someone we can't see.

I don't know when the picture was taken. The women are elegant, felt hats and gloves, the men wear jackets. My mother's wearing a light blue dress that skims her knee, and on her chest is draped a wide lace collar that hides her bare shoulders. Her longish hair tells me she's about eighteen, before my birth, before her life escapes her.

Everyone looks happy in the picture, the faces are proud, heads held high, and my future mother seems light.

I've often imagined there's a sort of counter, like the box office in a concert hall, or at the bank, where I might have been exchanged for freedom. I wonder what ID they asked her for when she came back to get me, and whether she recognized me when she saw me, or if she had a doubt, if she thought that maybe they had given her the wrong baby. I wonder how she reacted, if she smiled or cried, tears of despair or joy, relief or pride, or if her face remained impassive, if she was staggered by this other life for which she was now responsible. I don't know if her parents came inside with her or if they were waiting somewhere else, in the car parked out front, in the street, or in a parking lot around the side, if they were afraid of being seen, if they hid.

My mother fell in love and got pregnant. Her pregnancy was a fall, and, once at her lowest, who else could she call but her parents to come to her side? How would they have looked at her, and what would she have shown them? I don't know if they took her in their arms, or if they held me, my grandmother cradling me confidently in the crook of her arm, if they stayed back for a time coddling their bitterness, or whether the ice melted immediately when they saw the child.

I don't know how much my mother suffered, whether it was a real heartache the way they always are, when you're twenty and it's the first time and you think you're going to die. I wonder if he was nice. What colour his eyes were, his hair. Was he tall. Was he tender. What language did he speak. What were his interests. What did he do on his days off. What were his hobbies. What was the story of his life. Did he have secrets. Did he believe in God. When was he born. Was he charming, smart, happy, snarky, blasé, distant, manipulative, cruel, violent. Did she want to make love with him. Was it her first time. Did it hurt, did she bleed. Did she think that night about her parents, did she feel guilty doing what she shouldn't. Was she ashamed of herself. Was she afraid to go home, panic welling up inside her, did she want to run away, was she afraid to die, to suffocate. And when she got home, did they make her pay, was there screaming, did they let her have it, or was it merely sighs and long silences. Did her parents see right away that her body was changing, her belly swelling, or did she try to hide it. Did she realize right away, did she tell them early on or did she wait a few months, did she make love with him again knowing that the harm was done or did she do it again not knowing, or pretending not to know. Did she try everything so that the embryo

83

wouldn't stick, jump, run, dance, stop eating or eat junk, anything to start bleeding again, or did she hope it would disappear magically without doing anything, as if not thinking about it would make it not true, as if not thinking about it had the power to change reality.

But it was too late and soon it would be impossible to hide, and she would get kicked out of the house, evicted, expelled in order to rub out the stain, expunge the shame. I don't know if she left by herself, on the bus, with her suitcase, if her brother came to get her or whether her parents drove her, the drive quiet, her mother looking out the window, never turning her head toward those inside the car, her father smoking at the wheel. Whether they welcomed her, comforted her. What did she do all day, how did she keep busy, did she go out, how long was she there before she changed apartments, was the second place far from the first, was she comfortable, did she cook for herself, was she bored, did she read, did she go to the movies, did she watch TV, did she rub her belly or pretend it wasn't there, was she nauseated when she got up in the morning or all day long and did she tough it out like a penance. During all that time did she wait for her lover to change his mind and come back, did she dream that one day he would reappear and that they would start over, or start for real this time, or did her heartbreak feel final, her pride too wounded, was her anger taking up all the room, her pain less like a breakup than a sharp humiliation, and when she lay back on the stretcher was she already deep into resentment, wrestling with the harsh truth.

The day the pains started, how did she go to the hospital, did someone go with her, was it her brother and did he stay with her while she suffered, when the nurse told the young twenty-year-old girl alone without her mother that this pain was nothing, that what was to come would be much worse, like the evil fairy Carabosse cursing her, convinced that the young girl must pay. How did the labour start and when did they decide to put her under, after how many hours, and did she feel that pressure deep in her body that says it's time, it has to come out now because you can't take it anymore and you would do anything for it to stop even rip open your entrails. How much time went by between the anaesthetic and when she woke, before they put the child in her arms, that baby she would become aware of only after a time, after the lull of sleep, a white sheet draped over the moment the bodies came apart, as if it hadn't really come out of her or wasn't really her baby.

How did she feel, did she love the baby immediately, a little bit or more than life or did she hold back, distant, half absent, because she didn't yet know what she was going to do, was she still undecided, did she already know she couldn't keep it, not now, and she didn't yet know when or how. Did she know that at that moment her brother was speeding to Montreal and back in a blizzard, risking his life in the whiteout to go tell his parents they would never see him again if the baby was put up for adoption, and did she know that it was her father's brother, her uncle, who ended up forcing the decision. Who told her about the orphanage right near the hospital where she had just given birth, did she know about it already or did the nurse suggest it, did someone go with her or did she go by herself, did she cry or feel relieved, was she afraid or ashamed, did she tremble, did she go cold inside. Were the nuns kind, understanding, did they reassure her or did she once again feel like she was playing with fire, tempting fate. Did she stand in front of the building before going in, did she hesitate, did she want to run back up the stairs and get her baby or did she leave quickly without turning back. Did she see the inside of the place, the huge rooms full of cribs all in a row, and what did she do after, where did she go to regain her strength, was she in pain when her milk came in, did she wrap her chest, did she get groceries, did she look for a job, who did she talk to, whom did she ask for help. Did she sleep, eat, was it still snowing, did she cry.

When she got me back from the orphanage, when she took me back, when she chose me a second time for the first time, did she come looking for me among all the other babies, or did a nun bring me out, swaddled and bundled, into a waiting room or a vestibule, the room where the deliveries came, and the abandoned children?

In 1948, cast in the mother–daughter duo in *Ladies of the Chorus*, the girl who would become Marilyn Monroe held a doll of a newborn in her arms and sang, "Every Baby Needs a Da Da Daddy." In 1960, in *Let's Make Love*, she sang, "My Heart Belongs to Daddy."

One day, on a trip to Mexico, the actress, now famous, visited an orphanage. Before leaving, she wrote a check for a thousand dollars. Quickly, she tore it up and wrote out another, for ten thousand. They say that night was one of the rare times in her life when she fell asleep without pills. She usually made love standing up and in the light of day because she was afraid of the dark, she was afraid the night would never end. She said her father hadn't wanted to marry her mother and that was truly what had broken her heart. She also said that when you love a man and you tell him you're going to have his child, and he runs away, you never get over it.

It's Christmas Eve. The mother of the girl who will become Marilyn Monroe, Gladys, bears the name of her first husband Ed Mortenson as well as her own name, Baker, the name she gave her daughter Norma Jeane. After believing she was Mortenson's daughter, Norma Jeane learns at the age of five that the handsome dark-haired man on the only photo that hangs on the wall in her mother's room, the man who looks like Clark Gable, is her real father. His name is Stanley Gifford, and, much later, when the grown-up Marilyn Monroe calls him to introduce herself as his daughter, he answers through his lawyer.

He left Gladys after he got her pregnant, and, movie star or not, that child didn't count, the girl who, when she found out that man in the picture was her father, felt like she finally belonged to someone. Her first happy moment, she would say later, her first cinematic moment. She imagined coming home to her father, who had been waiting all along, a knight in shining armour, prince charming. She never found him, not in any movie and not in any of the actors with whom she starred.

I'm not writing a book about a mother with amnesia, about my lost father, about their unknown love story. I'm writing to fill in the blanks, to put words where there are none.

If my father had died instead of running away, if my mother had really truly abandoned me, I would feel like I have a story to tell instead of this fable I can't even consider legitimate because it's invisible. Nothing really happened, my mother came back, my father left, and I'm still alive.

Maybe we spend a whole life mourning, and maybe that's what I've done too, all my sorrows but not this one, I can't mourn what I don't know. This is the only disappearance I can't accept. I refuse to be that girl, a girl without a story.

If my father had died, I would have something left. If he had died, even before my birth, between the moment I was conceived and when I was born, that would mean he had lived. I would have been told about his death, and, maybe, to make things easier, they would have told me things about him. Even if he had taken his own life, I would have been fed some scraps of something and I could have constructed some idea of him, crafted him a face. Dead, he would have been harmless. But alive he was dangerous, alive and disappeared and threatening because there was always the risk he might come back, that he would claim me or reject me again, and do the same thing to my mother.

He never did, he stayed disappeared, and his disappearance became a holding pattern outside of time, a waiting with no end. He had been a thing unreal because it is never represented. If he had died, I could have filled in the blanks with items, with stories I would have been told, I could have sobbed without being able to stop and then my sadness would have made sense. We understand the pain of a child who's lost her father, it makes sense, it cancels out the silence, the suffering has a body. My father is without a body. He is a ghost, an empty, gossamer shell

I can run my fingers through. There are no images, he is the absence of absence.

How can you grieve something that hasn't been taken from you, or that you haven't been forced to leave, that has never been?

If he had died, I could weave him a shroud, and this book might be a burial of words.

Every bit of information is a fractal, each piece gives rise to hypotheses, calling to mind those tropical mangroves with roots that snake in every direction beneath the trees.

I often have the crazy urge to attack this text, to cut, empty, twist the words to bring them in line, force the narrative, corset the story, to do to these pages what I cannot do to my life. It enrages me not to be able to capture everything in a single image once and for all but my heart struggles against it, trips, my runaway heart, on a tear I can't stop, my heart will not rest.

There are so many questions, and all my life I've hesitated, I've asked myself so often if I shouldn't try harder to get interviews, find witnesses, retrace addresses and phone numbers, interrogate people, pencil in hand, dig through memories, demand my story, insist I be told the truth the whole truth nothing but the truth, but even under duress I couldn't. All that's left is a remix. I put on the headphones and listen to the beating of an irregular heart.

It's a story with no beginning or end. There's no such thing as the last word, that word which, once written, would set me free, because I'll never get to the end, once the last word has been put down I'll have to go back to the beginning, and this time, every time, because it's an impossible gesture, words will fail to render the nothing, and the nothing is also forbidden, it can't be thought, and even less written. Leave no trace, be guilty of nothing.

They say that children have to learn to manage their feelings. That's what we say from high up above and far away when we want everything except to share their tears, when we want them to soothe themselves. In return, children are faced too young with how alone they will be in life. Not solitary. Just alone.

I see my mother in her college uniform. She looks like a good girl in the blue and white. I don't know anything about that time in her life except what I rebuild, which is to say what I make up, image by image. My mother among her classmates, a starched, wimpled nun presiding from the end of the table. My mother on the phone, nestled into the couch, a cigarette between her fingers. My mother playing cards and drinking a bottle of Coca-Cola. My mother posing at the back of the garden. My mother surrounded by girlfriends with their hair blown out like ladies while hers is pulled back in a ponytail high on her head and tied with a ribbon. My mother laughing with her hair falling long to her shoulders, looking like Natalie Wood. My mother with short hair and thick bangs, like Jean Seberg. My mother thin and slight in the wide stripes of her Expo 67 cashier's uniform. My mother standing in an apartment with white walls, dried cattails on the floor, and, hanging from the ceiling, a fishing net hung with tchotchkes, pictures, starfish. My mother in a long light-pink dress on her graduation day, a flower in her hand and in her eyes something that looks like sorrow.

I'll never know which version she was, what she dreamed about, what thoughts went through her head while she was supposed to be studying, I don't know what she did for fun, what she thought about. I always believed that it was me who kept her from becoming who she was. Other times, I tell myself that baby opened up the world to her. But it's a palindrome, always the same. Forward or back, I come back to what I don't know. I turn the story over in every direction. I transpose, deduce, interpret, decode, I rewrite, I translate. I invent a secret lining for my secret.

Maybe I'll never know if what I know is true. But maybe one day there will be an apparition, a revelation, someone will snatch off the veil of doubt. And then I will be forced to let go of the only thing I do know, which is that I know nothing.

After my birth, my mother phoned him to tell him, and she told him the truth, words that were impossible to hear and that would change nothing. You have a daughter, she said. He replied that he would have preferred not to know even if it was already too late, that he might as well not have known because even if now he knew, he had already decided to leave and this didn't change anything, he was leaving.

I don't hear any hesitation in his voice. I tell myself that he laid things out very clearly, as if he were speaking to a stranger.

She would never see him again.

If I had been a boy, would the pain have been the same? If my mother had announced that he had a son instead of a daughter, would he have stayed? And if he had left, would my mother still have hesitated to keep me? How long would he have stayed? Would she have regretted it in the end? Would she have regretted years later not having decided to raise me on her own, to have lacked courage and now to be stuck with an unbearable creature, off-putting, remote, unpleasant, a man who would never have stopped leaving even while he stayed, abandoning her over and over again, in a pathetic apartment with a child he couldn't stand?

I don't know whether he announced he was leaving the city, the province, the country. I don't know if he really left, if he went elsewhere in Canada or moved to the States, or even to another neighbourhood in the city, I don't know if he went back to his country, the place my mother referred to as *back where he came from*, the industrial town in the Netherlands where he grew up. Maybe he spent the rest of his life on the run. Maybe he wasn't really an immigrant, maybe what he liked was staying a while without ever staying.

If he's alive, I'll never know where he lives, and if he's dead, I'll never know how he died, and if at the moment of death he saw the film of his life flash before his eyes, if he thought even for an instant of the daughter he never knew.

I'm not mad at him for leaving, for having chosen to live his life instead of looking after mine, and I can't get mad at him either for having made my mother suffer, because love affairs are what they are, especially at twenty. My only regret is that his absence has left me wrestling with breaches, strata, sediments, a world of ruins, the current, the undertow that will never leave me be.

I would have had to be a different person, or they would have had to tell me things differently, fewer secrets and a few more of those love stories we tell children so they can splice together the film of their origins. For that anguish to settle, and for me to be able to look ahead instead of twisting my neck around to try to glimpse the past, since we can never really see behind us anyway. Looking back will only ever be a gesture half completed.

I imagine a man for whom freedom has no price. The birth of a child, the arrival of a little girl, didn't fit with his vision of the future.

I imagine a venture capitalist, a CEO, never a politician, an artist or a writer, even less a police officer, never someone common, greying and beer-bellied, broke, maybe, a failure, lost, a loser, someone who scarcely existed. I see him alone on his deathbed, in a hospital room with no one around him, then I lie him in a coffin surrounded by a grieving crowd all in black. Sometimes I finish him off on a stainless steel stretcher, in the morgue, in an icy drawer. No one to claim him.

The images speed past, then I rewind as fast as I can and start over. His death never ends.

Every life is worth living, I know that, even mine. They say that no story is less important than another, that there's no hierarchy of suffering, and yet ... I've often regretted that I don't carry in my flesh a story that would give me the right to live with ghosts, permission to truly suffer, because real suffering is verifiable by facts. My story is a trite little story, an ordinary drama. The ghosts I live with have no glory, and, worse, in the grand scheme of things, they fall on the side of the conquerors, the rich, the powerful, the colonizers.

I was born at the wrong time, with the wrong skin colour, I've been ashamed to be white, pale, rooted in that slice of the world, ashamed not to have suffered a palpable pain, visible, measurable, ashamed to be living out a drama so private that it's a drama of privilege, and ashamed not to be able to heal, to return over and over again to the source of the story, my origin story. I can't close the file. The story stayed alive in me, a virus constantly reactivated. My shame was about my relationship to the world.

My mother was ashamed too, of what had happened to her, ashamed also to have shamed everyone. A shame she maybe eventually turned into pride, as she survived. If motherhood is a battleground, she won the war.

My mother was beautiful, alive, luminous, dazzling. I flip through old photos that look like paintings. Young woman in the bath, young woman asleep, young woman in the garden. She's always looking elsewhere than at the camera. She never meets my gaze.

My mother is a bastard in the story too, the forgotten one, abandoned, unnameable, the one who doesn't fit in anywhere, a grain of sand in the gears of everyday life. I can't even imagine how much she must have resented him.

I see again the turquoise eyes of my grandmother, pitiless, and I know that the love she had for me was tinged with her rancour for that stranger, everything I represented and she abhorred.

My father was a spotlight, a catalyst. He conjured up the image and then left, leaving in his wake the child, a reminder of him passing through.

In the end, there are four bastards in this story—my mother, my father, my grandmother, and me, four threads woven together, stories riddled with holes, stitched from throwaways, forgetting, wounds. Traumatized stories.

Back then they sometimes dragged men to court to force them to acknowledge their paternity and pay up. That was before welfare, when so much depended on the goodwill of men, the goodwill of families, and the help of the church.

If my father wasn't a father, is it because he was a stranger and it was better to see him go? Because he was so despised that to take him to court meant affording him more importance than he deserved? Or was it a question of pride, because either you love or you don't love enough, because love isn't something that can be forced, even if there is money to be had? Did he leave so fast that even if they had wanted to they wouldn't have been able to catch him?

My mother was determined: he had to disappear, at any cost, his passage in her life erased.

She told the nurse there was no father after I was born, no name to include on the document. The nurse insisted; my mother insisted. She told her flat out, looking the woman straight in the eyes, The father is me.

I don't know what she might have gotten from him if she had picked up that pen and dug the nib deep to carve his name, but maybe he would have had to do at least one thing, only one, admit that he and I were hyphenated, that it was true, I was his. And maybe then he would have carried some of the shame too.

That father, mine, never was.

My mother suffered a loss, and a betrayal, and an abandonment. In her mind, she was the one who was left, not me. If he left me too, it's because I was with her, I was a part of her, but it wasn't me as such, I didn't really exist, I wasn't yet somebody who could be left, I was simply an extension of her.

Perhaps my mother carried it all because she found herself like me, with a story aborted, a story that was over before I was even born. The love affair was over, the romantic horizon of youth. I stormed onto the scene in thick silence. Don't say anything, hide, hope that one day the humiliation will be forgotten by everyone. And above all, above all, don't show any pain, don't cry.

My mother, banished. My mother, abandoned.

My father is a made-up father. A father conjured up from silences that implied there was something to hide, that it was true. A father guessed at, the way you look at the night sky for the figures traced by the stars, a macabre constellation, the constellation of the deadbeat. He left, he made other children with other women and abandoned them like my mother. A black ghost, impossible to love, a dark, fearsome figure, someone you respect because you can't admire him. A man of marble or granite, straight and cold. A man all in black, or in green, military colours.

I remember a dream I had, a horrible dream, one night. I was thirty years old.

A Jeep roars through a city in ruins. It looks like a ghetto, the people dressed in rags, soiled, covered in thick dust, soot, their clothes worn through. They walk quickly, heads down to try not to be noticed, dodge the bullets of the snipers hidden on the rooftops and behind the rubble, avoid getting stopped by the officers. It's a grey day, the roads are covered in frozen mud, broken cobbles, the holes are full of frozen water, and the Jeep speeds through, parting to the sides of the road the bodies walking in the middle, slowly, skinny, weak puffs of breath from mouths dried by the winter cold.

I'm standing in the back of the Jeep, in a kind of box. I'm wearing the striped pyjamas. It's not important which war it is. I'm alone, the soldiers sit up front, machine guns in their hands. We are back to back, they are looking straight ahead, I'm looking behind me and holding on as tight as I can to prevent my body from falling out.

I don't know what I see, I don't know where they're taking me, I'm terrified. I have been chosen for some terrible thing, something that will happen to me or something I'll have to do. I don't know what awaits me. What I do know is that it's a grim assignation. The dream moves along with the Jeep, and I realize I'm being taken to a whorehouse where I will become the puppet of the sadistic commander. The truck rattles over the cobblestones. My body is thrown against the side of the box. I have no strength left. I am a dismembered doll. Everyone can see me, but no one looks at me.

After the Jeep, the dream cuts out, fades to black, and now I am on the bed, curled up in a tangle of sheets, used up, asleep.

When I woke up I remember thinking that I had just had a Nazi dream.

Maybe I was born of rape. Sometimes, often, I told myself that there was no doubt, I had been. There had to be an explanation, I wasn't sullied for nothing. I ended up telling myself the story of a very tall man who laid down above a tiny girl and who took her even when she said no, maybe she didn't say no because she didn't know how, she didn't say no because she had been taught that good girls listen and say yes even when the body resists, when anger wells up inside, injustice, the insistent refusal. When her strength gives out, she plays dead.

I couldn't fathom her desire, or her pleasure, as if shame couldn't have anything to do with the desire she had felt or the pleasure, despite everything that was forbidden, as if she couldn't possibly have been ashamed of it instead of giving in, and the shame I carried had to do not with rape, but joy, for which she had paid a hard price.

I long thought that he was mean, like the big characters in history or from the movies, one of those heroes you hate and admire the same time. I made him larger than life, stronger than anything, stronger than the woman who brought me into the world by herself.

Everything in my story pointed in that direction. Nothing I was told was good, that man represented nothing good, he had done bad things, he was ugly, he didn't speak French, he was an outlander to whom my mother had sold her soul or in whose arms she had lost it, and now, in exchange, there was me.

My father, gone like a thief. My father the dictator. My father the Führer. My father the Emperor. God my father. My father like the statue of the commander. My father absent. My father transparent. My father invisible. My father imperceptible. My father grandiose. My father like an eagle spiralling in the sky. My father the magnificent.

It isn't the absence of a father that makes a bastard. What makes a bastard is the secret.

It's not my father I am missing, my birth father. It's not that I'm suffering from not knowing once and for all whose blood runs in my veins. It's not that I suffered growing up raised by a young mother, which would mean that only a mom-and-dad life is worth living. That's not it. It's that my story has been erased, and, in the abyss of memory, I've tried all the words to fashion myself a father instead of a story. A straw man, a scarecrow.

Under the lead cloak I could imagine the worst. Why would they insist on such silence if not to hide something terrible? If no one was talking, that meant what had to be said couldn't be and I thought of all those Argentine children during the military junta, their parents tortured, assassinated, pushed out of airplane doors into the sea, five hundred babies taken and raised by torturers, their disdain and hatred against the murdered parents redirected against the living children, a private dictatorship.

Before the silence, dense, thick, so impenetrable, I struggled with my fear, the fear that things were unfolding in a blind spot and I couldn't see or only half guess by turning to catch some glimpse of what was happening behind me.

I remember all the images of women I surrounded myself with for years, everywhere I lived, postcards, posters, drawings tacked up on the walls around me, on bookshelves, always shown from the back or with their faces partially visible when they turned their heads to see what was happening behind them.

I placed myself behind these women's backs, I spent hours looking at them lovingly, hoping they would turn back toward me.

I sometimes imagine my father with a family, sitting at the head of the table, surrounded by his legitimate sons and daughters, having never said a word to them about me or about his other children sown here and there. In my mind he sits up very straight, his voice even while he speaks and they listen, their breath held, you could hear a pin drop. I don't know what he's talking about, if he's thanking the Good Lord or announcing some exploit, offering his blessing to a new couple or welcoming a new baby, offering his opinion of an important event, a political decision, an economic crisis. I always imagine him cultivated and intelligent, even if what I've been told about him, his work for a small design firm that subcontracted for Canadair, should bring to mind a man hunched over a drafting table, pencil in hand, doing what moves me more than anything, far more than philosophy or writing, the moving hand conjuring shapes on paper. Drawing.

If there had been a fairy at my baptism, I would have wanted her to grant me only one gift: to be able to draw.

I don't know why I think of him as a good family man. Deep down, I can't quite believe it, I don't really want to believe it, because that would mean accepting that he became the father of other children than me, children I've so often thought I might have crossed on the bus, on planes, in the metro, as I peered into faces looking for some resemblance, lost in my made-up stories, my way of believing that I wasn't alone in the world, stories I told myself so that I wouldn't jump up out of my seat and scream, scream out anything, let my anger loose and free.

Portrait of my mother as a young girl. She turns slightly and looks up toward the boy standing next to her, a boy a little bit older than she is, one who has done this often already and with who knows how many others before her, girls made for a boy like him, experienced, someone who's slept with a lot of girls and who intends to continue, often and with many, while this girl really likes him, the way you fall in love for the first time thinking it will also be last, that you'll never love like that again. Then I think of the boy's impatience, pushing the young girl away as you would wave off the annoying buzz of a mosquito.

This is not at all what he had in mind, trapped by an unwanted baby and a girl who doesn't want to get rid of it or let him go quietly. He didn't see this coming, and the girl either, except that she decided she would make it up as she went along. She refuses to walk offstage, stays put. She take up space, a squatter, she forces the dialogue, makes up lines and pushes the boy, who is no longer a boy but a man, to play his role even as he tries to flee, as he searches desperately for a way out.

He's a costume with no body, a role with no actor.

I take out the kraft paper envelope one more time. I've read and reread these notes countless times yet I remember nothing, it's like I've never seen them. There's the proof, I recognize the paper and the shape of the letters, these words are mine, but everything is strange, I don't quite believe it. Time has passed, and faced with these scratches I'm angry at myself for not doing anything, since I could have gone digging, I could have searched. It's like I didn't really want to find him at all.

Someone told me once that if I wanted it enough our paths would end up crossing and I would find him again by the grace of destiny. Either I didn't want it enough or else the law of crossing paths is more complicated than what mystics would have us believe.

I've often wanted to abandon this text, but that would have meant giving in to abandonment itself, and abandonment would have won. I would have given up, abdicated, surrendered to what I hate most, what scares me most and makes me most ashamed. Passivity.

My backaches regularly force me to lie down, to wait, wait, wait. The race has to be over, I'm in control again, I stay still while the pain eases and the spasms wear off, while my body capitulates. Movement stops, and thought stops with it. I don't read anymore, my head is empty, I lie on my back, curled up inside myself, swaddled.

This is the silent despair of those who grieve, the tears that wash everything away, empty out the sea, eroding the words.

This is not a book about my mother. It's not a book about my father either. It's a story about how there is no story.

I've told this story dozens of times, never the same way or to the same people, and never, really. I don't know if this time I'll get it right; this is it, then I'll never say anything again.

How many artists over the centuries have represented the angel Gabriel announcing to Mary that she would give birth to Christ? Her child too would be a bastard, and the story I tell is always and ever the same.

That time I went back to Rome to write but without being able to write, when I was fighting with the character of the young actress in a coma, I went out one day along the via Giulia, where the national Antimafia Commission is located, among the churches, palaces, the art galleries, and I walked to the criminology museum.

The via Giulia, with its discreet elegance and half light, is a narrow street between dark buildings that stand in contrast to the Rome of bright, warm colours. It reminds me of Florence. And there, set slightly back, is an old reform school.

The first room, with the torture instruments, feels menacing. What's stopping these objects from suddenly turning against me? What will they punish me with? An axe? A whip? A sword? Will they shut me in an iron maiden? Will I be accused of witchcraft? Locked in a dungeon? What crime have I committed? I look at the skeleton of that woman found deep in the palace, arms wrapped around her folded legs, her ankles and wrists bound, locked up by her husband in revenge for her love affair with another nobleman in the area.

In the final room, the fakes. I feel strange in front of the paintings hung on the walls, as if a second museum had been installed inside the first. It's impossible to know if the coins or Greco-Roman vases are originals or counterfeit. If everything is fake, then nothing is. Deep down, everything is real.

My father is a pitiless judge, the sword of Damocles always about to fall. He's the one I called up without knowing it in beloved faces because they were heaven-sent, those eyes that saw me, made me feel recognized, those lovers who without knowing it pulled me into a prison like sleeping beauty poised for her spindled sleep, hypnotized until I understood nothing at all, what was going on, what were people saying to me, what did they want from me, dizzy in the fog of contradiction, words so twisted that at one point I didn't even know how to read anymore, decode, I lost my bearings, was I losing my mind, tossed up and down on a teeter-totter, barrelling forward then running away, starting over, pushing back with all my strength against the slammed doors and the packed bags, the avalanche of cries, shattering words, the same scene on an endless loop, departure and abandonment, and resisting the secret belief that we deserved it, and which makes us stay, as if we were repeating history not because of a lack of willpower, but because there is a debt to pay.

I had one catastrophic love affair after another, and I came to believe that love just wasn't for me because I keep playing that first scene over again, the only one I've been told, the only one I'm able to imagine, that cinematic moment where one goes and the other stays, and that's what I've relived forever, the door closing behind someone who disappears again and again until either there's nothing left or else the reconstructed image is perfect.

The scenes are tumbling over each other. I'm writing like a spinning top or in a hurricane edging forward and tossing up everything in its path. I'm writing like a potter, throwing the clay to shape it until an object emerges from the long careful touch.

I'm impatient, I can't stand it anymore, collecting all the little pieces to organize them into the shape of the puzzle. I don't know what the picture is supposed to be, free-associating from the couch while I'm sitting in front of the screen. Writing opens up a landscape of ruins and this book is an orphan.

That night, when I was twenty, when my mother decided to talk to me, the night before I left, the brief moment when the veil was lifted and she revealed the only thing she thought she really knew about him.

That night, she told me that my father's father had murdered his wife—my father's mother—and that in jail he had taken his own life.

I don't know anymore if that's how she said it, with those words. Those are the words that come to me now.

Later, when I told the story to people I loved, I said, My grandfather killed my grandmother and committed suicide in jail. I said it like that, coldly, without any embellishment, brutal, as if it were banal, as if I wasn't moved, like it didn't concern me, when in fact I was astounded by my own words, I was slinging the words to hear their echo, and perhaps then I might believe them.

I don't know how old my father was when his father committed the crime. I don't know where it happened or why, or how. I don't know if my father was a witness or if it took place in his absence, behind his back. I don't know who took care of him after his father was arrested and how he reacted to the verdict. I don't know if my father was taken in by a member of the family or handed over to the state, or if that's when he left the country. I don't know how everyone else reacted, if my father's father was a violent man who beat his wife regularly or if on the contrary no one could have guessed. I don't know if the newspapers made that their headline, if classmates and friends turned away or if they were kind.

I know only one thing, which is that my grandfather, the other grandfather, the unknown grandfather, the grandfather so imaginary that he may as well have emerged from a novel, that he stood trial, was sentenced to life in prison, and, once he was behind bars, chose to end the life he had so poorly led.

There. That's what I know.

I don't know anything about my father, but I know this: his father was a murderer.

My grandfather killed his wife. He killed a woman. I am that man's granddaughter.

The night I stood with her in the guest room, my mother told me what I've kept tucked in my mind, re-markable and shameful, like a birthmark everyone stares at because you just can't hide it. My mother's words be-came a shocking secret, terrible, which I couldn't share even if it's all I had, and so that's what I did, I shared it with people who didn't really count or who didn't always count, people I was seeing or sleeping with, to whom I gave nothing else of importance, nothing but that story. To them I showed a part of me that was not me, but that might have been the only part of my life I could tell, the only thing a few sentences could hold, a screenplay where for once it was clear who was whom and who had done what.

I've told it without knowing each time why I was tell-ing the story of the murder my mother gave me, why I was doing it at that particular moment, why I felt the need, and what I was really saying at all. Maybe I wanted to see if it was true, because saying it makes the words sticky with reality. Maybe it was to make me the daugh-ter of that man, if not in real life then at least in a story, even if it meant becoming a kind of monster like him. The story hammered in the nail of shame. Between shame

117

and pride, as I found out, there is only one breath, a small, delicate sigh.

I told this story because it was unique and strange, the kind of thing that takes you aback, surprising. I told it because it seemed to come out of a novel or a movie, a made-up story like in a fairy tale. I cherished this bit of trivia in which I was a character by proxy, this story that was the draft of my life, the mockup. I knew nothing, I had nothing, but I had that.

A poisoned story: the one about the little boy whose mother, a tall, red-haired woman, flamboyant, sensual, and magnificent, is assassinated. He's ten years old, he doesn't know that one day he'll become a famous writer, that his detective novels will sell by the millions, be optioned by Hollywood, adapted for the big screen. But the boy will also become a voyeur, a pervert, a collector of affair after affair, romances, marriages, because he's looking for the woman who will be able to take the place of the woman who was taken from him, his greatest love, his mother. All his life he is haunted by his mother's murder. All his life he tries to solve the crime. He tells the story once, twice, three times, he sleeps with a lot of women, he sells a lot of books, the crime is still unsolved because numbers don't count, what counts is that fever dream, that passionate inquiry that gives a shape to his life, the shape of what eludes him, draws away then returns, the shape of what loops over and over, the identity of a single thought—recreating the scene of the crime.

What my mother told me that night in that room that belonged to no one etched itself into my genome. These are words that wrote me, and because they were the only words given to me, they took up all the room. It's by tracing over them today that I can rewrite the past, retrace how a few words, barely a sentence at most, and one I don't even know is true, dictated the way I see myself. Does my whole life hang in that one searing instant when my mother spoke those words? The pain, the suffering, the language my body has found to speak, does it all have to do with the fact that I'm writing them at this very moment, with this fever that's burning my forehead and my cheeks, the pain rising at the same time too, following the twist of my spine to lodge in the centre of the target, where fingers open and close into a fist, where an eagle hooks its prey in its talons and doesn't let go, the spot in my back opposite my heart.

They say: to be taken advantage of, to be taken for a ride.

My mother finally opened up because I was about to leave for months with my bag on my back. Airplane, train, bus, hitchhiking across Ireland and Corsica, along sharp escarpments, the absurd beauty that can't contain anything. The violence too, of a torn, passionate people.

I was leaving, and my mother was losing me, at least a little, maybe just enough. Is that why she suddenly wanted to tell me where I came from, she who had never told me anything? Did she tell me the way you slip a collar around the neck of a dog, so that I would know who I belonged to even if it told me nothing in the end, nothing true? Even if the name of that man was more or less a needle in a haystack, a name that wasn't even really a proper name, deep down, it was so common, and the first name that was a surname made up from an amputated first name, the last name that had blotted out the original first name.

She also told me the name of the city where he may have been born, telling me it was the city we had crossed once a long time before during a trip, I was very small, too small, the two of us weren't alone, her husband was with us, my new father, and also their child, the little girl born two years earlier and who from then on I could imagine in his arms like a blurry vision.

Father–daughter scenes don't move me. When I see them, I feel nothing, it's a language I don't understand. But I can't stop sobbing watching the trains pull out in front of the camp, when they separate the mothers and the children.

That time, when my mother saw the name of the city on the highway sign for the exit, she said nothing. She only turned to look at me on the back seat, asleep.

I imagine she was trembling, something inside her was set in motion, freeing her padlocked memory. I imagine her stomach in knots. Maybe her eyes misted over. Maybe her chest tightened at the windmills and the thought that a part of me is from there.

My mother couldn't know that I would always feel caught in the crossfire, I would never really belong to anyone, to any place, maybe not even to myself.

Everything has been leading me here, and now that I'm here, something's starting to give. I am watching the scene of the grandparents and the scene of my mother in the downstairs bedroom and the scene with the desk where I'm writing in my room today. The pages pile up and now my arms are feeling it. My left shoulder is on fire as I wrench at the words. I search for the words and a sharp pain interjects, a safety catch. My arms are falling off, I can't write anymore, they can't carry anything. A phantom pain, sadness always hidden and lying in wait for permission to show itself. My body a door open on the past. Calcified, ripped from the bone by a shock, the spur courses through my body, paralyzing my arm in pain that paradoxically is a sign of healing, as tiny stones are reabsorbed by the flesh. I am a chipped pillar of salt. I turned to look behind me. Something is crumbling.

Only once did I go back to my mother to ask her directly to repeat what she had already told me, to tell me once more, reassure me that I wasn't inventing it to make myself interesting or to create the man who had left. I hadn't stolen the plot from a novel or a movie, this wasn't a scrap of nightmare or a waking dream. I asked my mother to confirm what my father had told her.

I asked her to tell me again so that I could see something more clearly. I needed to face what I was going through at the time, a love affair that was tearing me apart piece by piece.

I had fallen in love, I had fallen head over heels, I was falling. The princess had turned into a toad and then a monster, from devotion to rejection to scorn, from love to jealousy. I had become the screen on which hatred, behind the mask of love, was being projected. The doors of a heart I thought I had locked forever had been thrown wide open, and I was paying for it. I had fallen in love with someone like me, branded by shame and illegitimacy, and instead of healing I was going to succumb.

Both illegitimate, she and I had found each other, but our alliance had become a war, it was all meant to erase me, exhaust me, to take me for everything, even my story, to occupy space and time, fill them with words and cries until I couldn't think. To destroy each part of what had been my identity, little by little, so deeply, until I didn't want to write, until I disappeared, until I ceased to exist.

In one of those moments of intimacy that made me believe in love, I had told her about the father, the grandparents, the murder, and later, in a slyly recycled intimacy, after she had hit me, she had rendered her judgment: deep down, I'd gone looking for it. I had wanted us to act out the scene again, the scripted violence dictated by the past.

Her words sealed our fate. I took off the ring and cut all ties to end the spiral into madness. Months later, when the soul had stanched its bleeding, I wondered whether she was onto something.

If I had recreated anything, it was maybe my mother's big love for an immigrant they said was in Quebec against his will. He spoke English, he didn't like French-Canadians and maybe not even Montreal or the New World. He had disappeared just as he had arrived. Outlander.

Today I've forgotten almost everything except the structure of the story, and the feeling of suffocating, a fist around my heart, the sharp sensation of being trapped, the fear, the despair that the insidious violence might remain invisible, that stealthy, hidden violence, and especially the shame to have found myself there, to have lived a love like that.

I was ashamed to have loved so much and so blindly. I was ashamed to have been trapped and to have fallen into it softly, as into a faint. I was ashamed of carrying inside me, on me, under my skin, stories about a murdered grandmother and a grandfather in jail, and the story of their son too, a contemptible man who did not become my father. My train wreck of an affair had revived them all, and I was all of those stories.

I came out of it like surfacing after drowning.

I long thought it was my real father, the flesh and blood, that I was looking for. I know now or I think I know that the man who existed, the one they call in spite everything my *father*, has nothing to do with it, he doesn't count.

My life has not been without men, and I didn't mourn my lost father every time I left them. I didn't replace him with anyone, the men or the women I've loved, except by falling in love with people who are larger than life, since who can measure up to absence if not someone who takes the space we give them, all of it, completely?

But no one was missing from my life, at least not a man, and not that man. Rather, I had to break the spell cast by an imaginary father, an unreal, all-powerful, supernatural father, one I was forced to obey because from where he was inside me, he could do only two things, watch and punish.

Now everything is possible, now I can imagine everything, a Fascist grandfather and a Jewish grandmother, a wife beater and his victim, a romantic betrayal and a cuckolded husband, an erotic game gone wrong, a crime of passion, an incurable disease and the ultimate reprieve, a crime of compassion, drugs, fists, a rope, a pillow, a gun, poison, a blade, a moment of madness, a broken heart. I can say what I want. Maybe it's a way to make them appear, the way you smoke out rats to force them to come out, to catch them.

I haven't lost hope that my mother will remember or that someday I'll find out that my father isn't dead, that he'll reappear to explain, amend, tell me what I've been told is wrong or else someone will come to me who knew him, his son or his daughter or a friend from that time will come to me with those long-awaited words. One day I might receive a letter, which I would open delicately so as not to damage anything, and I would read it like a novel. I imagine this without ever thinking that the words might be devastating, the man could be a liar, I never think I might regret it, because words can't be worse than silence. Nothing could hurt me as much.

Maybe I've refused to write the story for so many years to try to keep it intact, preserve the little I had for fear that in telling it I would make it disappear forever, white within and beyond, and then nothing would have existed at all. The case would be closed and I would lose both the story and the father for good, the father and those fictions I spin to fill the void, made-up stories that give my life meaning.

If I lost that father, even the idea of him, the imaginary father, would I lose myself too? Would I disappear?

One night—I'd already begun to write this story—my mother hands me a sheaf of paper, letters she found cleaning out closets or drawers that had been shut for a long time. She hands me letters she kept—my mother, who throws everything away, my mother who has never kept a single thing. With the little lamp behind me spreading its halo against the wall, I unfold the sheets, the handsome curlicued handwriting.

My mother is twenty years old, she is pregnant, she is alone in the apartment my uncle found for her in Quebec, she's writing letters to two young women, girls she's never met but corresponds with. There is no one to talk to here and my mother tells her story to two strangers—her lost love, the child who will soon be born.

I'm forty-five years old, the sentences are in front of me, I fill in the blanks. I imagine what my mother wrote to elicit these replies. I tell myself she recounted her parents' anger, my grandfather's disappointment, my grandmother's rage, she described her isolation, she didn't belong anywhere anymore and she said she didn't know yet what she was going to do with me since the letters tell her that maybe now's not the time to make a decision, maybe she could consider finding a nanny to look after the baby for the first few months instead of putting it up for adoption right away, maybe she should wait for the grandparents to see the child and hope the walls come down, their defences, the resentment, hope their heart melts.

I decipher them, I develop the words like the negatives of a photograph, I turn the sentences inside out like a glove.

A few months later, over a year after having filled out and mailed the document, an envelope arrives in the mail. Inside, a few wisps on four stapled sheets of paper, with the file number 35,953. I wonder if the number represents how many children were put up for adoption at the time, thirty-five thousand children abandoned for a time or for good.

On December 16, 1968, forms were filled out, information about the mother, the father, as in every adoption, two chirpy profiles, two *sensible* and *talented* young people, *good-looking*, *artists*. He has three brothers and a sister, his parents have passed away. He left school at fourteen and has been in night school since to become an engineer. I wonder how old he was when he arrived in Montreal, how long he stayed, and what he did between the death of the parents and his departure, and where his brothers and sister went, if they also immigrated here or if they went back. I don't know what to do with the blue eyes and the blonde hair, I don't know if the qualifiers *gentle* and *kind* that describe the father are my mother's words or those of the nuns who wanted to improve the baby's odds. Because who would adopt the abandoned blood of a monster?

I'm eight years old, ten, twelve. The fits lasted a few years—I would suddenly start shaking and fall to the floor, stiff and wracked, my eyes rolling back in my head. I was afraid. I was afraid of what was happening and also of the people I found bent over me when I woke, the audience for the spectacle I was making of myself.

To suffer from not being seen, and suffering just as much to know you're being watched. To think that existence has to do with being recognized, and being forever afraid of being unmasked. Worrying that it's obvious: my birthmark; my body, marked.

Deep down I am still that child abandoned and then retrieved whose existence was waiting for the gaze of others, little mismatched thing.

In the world in which I was born, it was possible to be a bastard. Today, fatherless children are neither demon nor divine, and women who raise their children alone are just single. But the children robbed of a story, the children cloaked in secrets, empty of words, they might stay forever bastards. They are dogs without collars, beings who learn to cower, who turn their tongue a hundred times in their mouth before speaking because they always feel like they're barking in a foreign language. Creatures caught somewhere between I love yous, I love you nots, I don't love you enough, I cannot love you.

That night, in the downstairs bedroom, the white basket at her feet, clothing and sheets waiting to be folded, when I asked my mother if she had a picture of him, when she lowered her head and muttered that she had one but tore it up, I felt an abyss open up. It was a loss, my heart was broken.

Still today I catch myself dreaming that they had a great love story. A forbidden love, a secret love, a love against all odds.

The words I would have liked to hear about my parents: they were in love, or: we loved each other.

I've often dreamed of writing a book with an ending that would give me back the first days of my life. Searching, questioning, harassing, at the end of my research I would finally have found him. I would knock on his door or arrange a meeting without telling him who I am, in a restaurant or café, in the hospital, on his deathbed, and there he would be, before me, no longer able to hide, he would appear.

I don't know what we would say to each other. I hear only silence, it's an impossible script to write. What do you say to someone after a whole life has gone by? How can you catch up after all that time? What would I say about myself if someone asked me to tell them everything from the start? What would I reply if they asked me who I am? Nothing, or else a lie.

Or else. After so many years my mother one day will hand me an envelope with a handwritten letter, a letter written in his hand saying he loves her and he loves the child just born but he cannot stay, he is drawn away, he's afraid of doing them more harm than good, both to her and to the child, he knows he's fragile, unpredictable, he's toxic and she has to believe that if he leaves it'll be for the best. At the end, he asks her not to destroy the letter though he knows how angry she is. He asks her to keep it, along with a picture of the two of them, the only image that remains, for later, if she wants, when their daughter will be grown.

Or else. Out of nowhere, an already elderly man will approach me, a little hunched over, he's past his prime, he introduces himself, hand held out. I don't immediately catch his name, and when I do it doesn't ring a bell, strange sounds, I ask him to repeat it. Then he says that name again, pronounces it clearly and this time I hear it, clearly. I see he is looking at me, his eyes patient, not worried or troubled, a kind of neutral benevolence. I look at him, and though I've never seen him I recognize him, I see myself in his eyes. Time is suspended, and the scene stops there.

There's no sequel. It's an impossible meeting, just like the story is impossible to write. It's an empty dream, a hollow nightmare.

I reread a few lines, I cut entire pages, I slice through flesh, muscle, nerves, I try to reach the heart, bone, I feel like I can't. What I say is never enough and always too much, I can never find the right words.

By want of courage, sometimes, I withdraw for days or weeks, huddled in my living room or in the anonymity of another city, a foreign city, I write in silence, I write because there's nothing else to do, because when you have no story the only thing that's left is to invent one, like children who suddenly begin to doubt and invent incredible origins or famous parents. I don't know why I'm writing if not to replace the emptiness with words that aren't anything either but at least they furnish the space left empty.

Sometimes I hear myself say it's over, I won't write anymore, it's futile, it's useless suffering, a game of patience that changes nothing, it especially doesn't heal and if anything makes the pain sharper still, an autopsy conducted not on a cadaver but on life itself.

But then, riveted to the screen of my own history, each time I start again, and I give in.

I only exist when I'm writing, or when, for a moment, I feel the ache to end it, and then the urgency of survival.

I'm twenty years old. Twenty years after the room at the Jeffery Hale, I spend the last nights of the long trip after that conversation with my mother in a little studio in the centre of Brussels with a Brazilian musician I met on the train.

Our eyes catch between the bodies of the police officers checking papers, who pay very little attention to me, the tourist, and far too much to him, the immigrant, who is sitting across from me.

After they've gone, a bit of banter, a laugh, he tells me about his long-distance love with a German publicist, and I must have revealed pieces of my life. Today, as I'm writing, I no longer remember what I told him. All I know is that he was alive.

It's the day before I go home, this boy will be my last risk, walking in a city in the middle of the night, hitch-hiking, following strangers. Maybe I played with fire, tempted fate, to see if the past would repeat itself. Maybe I wandered from room to room to see if I might finally get lost, leave my own life, but I didn't disappear, and I did not try to find the man who has not been my father.

The boy offers to put me up. I go home in three days. The last night, he's sitting near me on my makeshift bed on the floor of the room where I've spent the last two nights awake, watching the sign from the shop next door blink its lights against the white ceiling. I am an insomni- ac, flustered by time running between my fingers, specks of freedom.

I don't know why, but that night, all of a sudden, we're both giddy, with a crazy, light joy, our bodies and clothes tangled without trying to make it pretty and without playing at romance. I watch us as if this were a movie and our roles were played by actors, amazed by how bodies fit together, by the precision of our gestures.

I shared with no one the details of that night, I kept them to myself, like a talisman. Nothing changed, and yet—.

When I thought about it again, afterward, every time, the words that came to me were the same I scribbled on a piece of paper on the plane on the way home. Something tender and pornographic.

The young woman in love with a stranger is me.

The one who leaves her baby at the orphanage is me.

The young woman wandering in the streets of Quebec City, head down before an invisible horizon, powerless, is me.

And I am the woman with amnesia, fallen, injured, the woman curled up asleep.

I am all of these women.

That was the promise of my actress character. The young woman who preoccupied me, who haunted me. The one from whom I turned away after circling around her without understanding why or knowing how to shake the obsession. As if I were waiting for the fiction to wake her. Or for her to wake me.

In the end I abandoned her, something gave way, I started over, though without really going very far. In the end I stayed next to her, right up close. That's when this book was born, the book you're holding, in the middle of a storm.

When everything was white out.